THE PACT

"You've been hanging around Quinn's crazy ass too long." Raven Montgomery stared at her friend, Ava for a full minute before scanning the shocked faces of Mac and Ryleigh. Of course, Quinn had a smile on her face as wide as the lake, asking us to hear Ava out. *Baby Bump Boot Camp? Who comes up with that kind of crap anyway?* Raven always loved coming home to Rosewood Heights, especially if it meant hooking up with all of her besties. This was just supposed to be a Sunday afternoon christening for Ava's baby boy, a nice small reception at Rosewood Estates, and a few laughs with her girls. Not. Another. Damn. Challenge. She looked at the two drinks in either hand—a mango mojito in one and Crown Vanilla and cream soda in the other—and couldn't decide which she should drink first. Raven settled for the latter and took a huge gulp. She waited for Mac and Ryleigh to say something. *Anything.* But they looked just as shell-shocked.

Finally, Ryleigh said, "Hell. No."

"*Yes! My girl.* I second that!" Raven lifted her glass in mock toast.

"So why don't we hear her out?" Quinn asked, hope glimmering in her eyes. Again.

Raven threw up her hands. "Quinn, why? Didn't you just hear us? No. Just. No." She could handle just about anything, but the thought of motherhood scared her to death. She heard Bryson laugh and glanced over to where he stood with all the guys. She knew her husband would be all in for this challenge, and that he would make a wonderful father. It had been a little over five years since he'd started the youth center and she loved watching him interact with all the kids. She loved watching him period.

Raven came back to the conversation and heard Mac say, "Just like we tuned your ass out when you initially mentioned this challenge to us, we plan on doing the same to her."

But Ava ignored them all and paced in front of them as she explained the details of *Baby Bump Boot Camp*, which was supposed to help you get that bun in the oven and show you ways to lose the baby bump afterwards. The camp started on Wednesday and lasted through Saturday, with each day having a different theme. She remembered the pamphlet Quinn had given them at her wedding reception, which Raven had promptly stuffed in her purse without looking at it. She still hadn't read it. Actually, she had no idea where she'd put the thing. This was not how Raven planned to spend her week of vacation. She had envisioned long, leisurely walks in the garden, sunsets at the lake and passionate nights with her sexy husband.

"I'll take the class."

Wait. What? Raven whipped her head around and stared openmouthed at Mac.

"But don't expect me to try and have a baby afterwards. I can't commit to that," Mac continued.

EMBRACING EVER AFTER

ONCE UPON A BABY SERIES (BOOK 1)

SHERYL LISTER

Editor: Nicole Falls, Silent N Publishing
Design: Sherelle Green

To Having Best Friends

ACKNOWLEDGMENTS

My Heavenly Father, thank you for my life and for loving me better than I can love myself.

To my husband, Lance, you will always be my #1 hero!

To my children, family and friends, thank you for your continued support. I appreciate and love you!

To my sisters of the heart, Leslie Wright, Sherelle Green and Angela Seals. Love you to life!

Nicole Falls, you are a LIFESAVER!! Love you, girl!

Thank you to all the readers who have supported and encouraged me. I couldn't do this without you.

DEAR READER

Dear Reader,

Raven, Quinn, Ryleigh and Mac are back, along with another Best Friends Challenge! It's definitely going to be an interesting ride, especially when it may include diapers, pacifiers and bottles. I had such a blast collaborating with Sherelle, Angie and Elle, once again, and can't wait to do it again. For the best reading experience, we recommend reading the series in order. You can thank me later. Enjoy!

Love & Blessings!
Sheryl

sheryllister@gmail.com
www.sheryllister.com

"If you don't get pregnant within a year, the next girls trip is on you. And it won't be cheap!" Quinn said.

Raven couldn't believe her ears. Mac *caved*. But she wasn't the only one shooting daggers at her friend. Ryleigh had the same glare on her face. Quinn squealed and her smile matched Ava's. Both knew that if one of us agreed, we all would, even if it was done reluctantly.

Ava smiled her way. "Raven?"

"I knew one day we'd take this Best Friends Challenge stuff too far. I mean, getting married was at the top of the list of the craziest shit we've ever done. But this right here, ladies, takes it to an entirely new level." She groaned, finished off the Crown and cream soda, then followed it with a swig of the mojito. *Ugh! They've got me out here cussing and drinking like Mac and Ryleigh.* She reluctantly held up the glass. "Fine. This is the last time." She was getting way too old for these challenges.

Ava prompted Ryleigh and Ryleigh slowly lifted her glass after nudging Mac to do the same.

The moment their glasses touched, Raven felt like she had just signed her death warrant. Her stomach knotted and her chest tightened. She couldn't do this. Sure she helped Bryson and their other two friends, Jerome and Kendrick with the annual camping trip Bryson held for the kids at his youth center, but that was only for a couple of days. A little hike, meal preps and a few games, then back to their parents. At one time, she had thought about having children. She and Bryson had even discussed starting a family soon, but she had steered away from the conversation as of late.

"Hey, baby."

Raven jumped slightly. She hadn't even heard Bryson approach. "Hey."

Bryson studied her and frowned. He ran a comforting hand down her spine. "You okay?"

Not ready to tell him about the latest challenge, she smiled brightly and leaned up to kiss him. "Fine. Let's go for a walk."

"You sure? I thought you wanted to spend time with your girls."

"We did, and now I want to spend time with you." And she needed a few minutes. She was a heartbeat from a shutdown, the way she always dealt with being overwhelmed. After a round of quick hugs, Raven excused herself from her friends. She and Bryson started a slow stroll away from the group of people still milling around oohing and ahhing over Little Sully, as they called the baby, and his two-year-old sister, Madison. She threw up a wave to Ava's parents when they passed. As they continued walking deeper into Love's Last Garden, she felt her tension begin to subside. Raven took a deep breath and the various floral scents filled her nostrils. Bryson grasped her hand. His mere touch calmed her further. Being with him had always relaxed her. Their steps slowed when they reached the long fence. Whenever a couple got engaged or expressed their love in the garden, they placed a lock on the fence. Each time she came home, she saw more and more of the small metal pieces, some plain and some with intricate designs and bold colors.

Bryson took a few steps and stopped at the lock he'd presented to her, the one they'd placed on the fence together. "I can't believe it's been almost three years."

"Me, either." Raven fingered the small silver lock with their names engraved on it and a smile curved her lips. Her relationship fears and insecurities had gotten the best of her and she'd run away from him. From them. But he'd come after her, proposed to her and made her the happiest woman in the world. After being best friends since college, their whirlwind love affair had taken them both by surprise. Earlier she'd said that the marriage pact had been one of the craziest Best Friends Challenges, but she'd lied. There was nothing crazy about the way she loved Bryson, about how she looked forward to his face being the first thing she saw every morning, or how they could talk for hours about everything and nothing. There was nothing crazy about the way he could turn her on with just one look, or the way he touched her, kissed her, and made love to her. No, it wasn't crazy. It was perfect. *He* was perfect for her.

He wrapped his arms around her waist and nuzzled her neck. "What are you smiling about?"

She turned in his arms and stared into his whiskey-colored eyes. "You. Us. And how much I love you. Thanks for being my very best friend and for loving me the way you do, Bryse. These last three years have been nothing short of incredible."

"They have, and it's only going to get better." He caressed her cheek, then slanted his mouth over hers in a deep, passionate kiss.

Raven moaned as his tongue twirled slowly around hers, tasting, teasing, claiming what was his. She slid her arms around his neck and pressed her body closer to his, feeling his growing erection against her belly.

It was his turn to groan as he trailed kisses along her neck and shoulder. "Baby, I'm about two seconds from laying you down and making love to you right here."

"Hmm, you think we could get away with it?" She wondered if this was one of the places on Mac's list of public places to have sex that Mac had promised to give Raven.

Bryson's head came up sharply. "Don't tempt me."

"Who me?" she asked innocently, running her hand over his engorged length.

He clamped down on her hand. "We need to keep walking before you get us both in trouble."

Raven chuckled and shrugged. "If you say so."

He shook his head and grabbed her hand. "Come on. Besides, I need to know what's bothering you. And before you try to say it's nothing again, remember I *know* you."

She sighed. Yeah, he knew her better than she knew herself most times. He'd always been able to read her and know when she had something weighing heavily on her mind. And this latest challenge was doing exactly that. She didn't say anything for the first few minutes, and he didn't press. He just waited like he always did, giving her the time and space she needed. It was one more thing she loved about him. They stopped near the lake and she stared out over the water. "It's another one of those Best Friends Challenges Quinn talked us into, and this time, she even got Ava on board."

Bryson laughed softly. "Hey, the last one turned out to be good for me, so I'm not mad at her. What is it this time?"

Raven hesitated briefly, then said, "A baby."

"Wait. Are you saying the challenge is to see who can have a baby first?"

"No, just like the last time, we're all supposed to be pregnant within a year. Crazy, huh?" When he didn't respond, she turned to face him.

A slow grin curved his lips. "Hell, no. I'm down for this one, and ready to win! We're going to be first."

Of course he was. The excitement in his eyes reminded her of a kid who'd just been told he was getting his favorite toy for Christmas. As much as she didn't want to, it was hard not to get caught up in his enthusiasm and she found herself smiling, too.

He placed a gentle hand on her stomach. "I can already imagine how beautiful you'll be pregnant with our baby."

Whoa! Morning sickness, swollen ankles and looking like a beached whale didn't meet her definition of beautiful. It sounded more like being miserable and uncomfortable. "There's more."

He raised an eyebrow.

"She also roped us into doing this *Baby Bump Boot Camp* thingy." Raven still couldn't believe Mac was the first one to agree. She was supposed to be the strong one, the hell-no-I'm-not-doing-that-shit one, but, *nooo*, not this time. This time, she'd surrendered. Raven felt another round of curse words working their way through her. She took a deep breath.

"Ah, a what kind of camp?"

"You heard me." She repeated all the information Ava had given them.

"And this thing lasts four days."

"Yeah," she grumbled. She was going to fly to Quinn and Paxton's home in Memphis and burn every magazine, book and article Quinn had in her possession. Knowing Paxton, he'd probably supply the matches.

Bryson seemed to be thinking. "Okay. I'm in. We're going to win this thing, baby." He must have noticed her lack of enthusiasm because he asked, "What are you worried about? You're going to be a great mother."

Her ex's caustic words replayed like a broken record in her head. She shoved them aside and pasted a smile on her face. "I'm not worried," she lied.

"Good. I think we should start now. Did I tell you how much I love this dress you're wearing?"

His fingers slid beneath the thin shoulder straps on her sundress and he backed her slowly towards the large oak tree. "Um...no." Raven didn't particularly like wearing dresses. She preferred jeans, sweats and T-shirts, but since he liked them, she had made a concerted effort to wear them more often. Her back hit the tree. She briefly wondered again if this was on Mac's list. If not, she might share it with her. Then again, maybe not. This was *her* special place with Bryson. The place where she let go of all her fears and embraced their love. The place where he made all her dreams a reality as they said "I do." Raven decided that she'd keep this one to herself.

"Well I do. A *lot*. Do you know why?" he asked, easing the straps down and freeing her breasts.

She didn't know how he expected her to answer with his mouth kissing, sucking and licking all around her breasts, and his hand beneath her dress moving her panties aside. She heard the slide of his zipper.

"It shows a lot of leg just the way I like and makes it easy to do this." He entered her with one long thrust. "No time like the present to get started on the challenge."

Raven's head fell back as the intense sensations took over. She locked her legs around his waist, taking him deeper inside of her. This she could do. But the challenge, she planned to lose. Forever.

BABY BUMP BOOT CAMP

Raven awakened Wednesday morning to Bryson idly stroking her thigh, something he often did throughout the night, as if assuring her she was safe, that he would be there. And she did feel safe with him, always had. No matter what had happened, she could always count on him. Raven did her best to assure him of the same thing—that he could count on her to be there for him. She peeked over at the clock on the nightstand. Thank goodness they still had a couple of hours before the boot camp started. It would give them time to go downstairs to the Rosewood Inn's restaurant and have breakfast. Those waffles were calling her name. Last night, Quinn had sent out a text to all of them as a reminder not to be late. *More like to make sure they were all still going to partici-pate*, she thought with a wry grin. If Raven could come up with a way to wiggle out of the thing, she would in a heart-beat. But no such luck. Sighing, she snuggled her naked body closer to Bryson, her back against his front, and closed her eyes. Minutes later, her eyes popped open and she gasped as Bryson's touch changed. The caresses became more deliberate, more sensual until she was writhing against him. She felt his thick erection growing harder against her butt.

"Wh…what are you doing, Bryse? We have to get ready for…*ooh.*"

"We have time," Bryson murmured, lifting her leg over his and trailing his hand up her inner thigh. He placed butterfly kisses along her neck, shoulder, and upper back.

Raven shuddered when his fingers slipped inside and began stroking her. He probed deeper and she moved her hips in time with his rhythm. Her breaths came in short gasps, and her legs trembled. She arched her head back, closed her eyes and bucked against his hand, crying out wildly as an orgasm ripped through her. Before she could recover, he rotated his fingers and did something that seized her body with a rush of sensation so intense she thought she might pass out. Her eyes flew open, her body went rigid and she came again. Bryson withdrew his fingers, tilted her hips and entered her with one thrust. She didn't think she'd ever get enough of making love with him. The slow slide of his shaft in and out of her rekindled her still simmering passion all over again. "I love the way you feel inside me."

"And I love the way you feel, sweetheart."

He brought his hand up to caress her breasts, then traveled down her belly to her clit. He circled the bud slowly in time with his strokes. Electricity shot from her core and flared out to every part of her body. "*Bryse!*"

"I'm right here." He groaned and increased the pace. "You feel so good, I'm tempted to keep you here all day."

Yeah. All day is good. She reached back and grasped his butt, pulling him closer and forcing him to move faster. She used her feminine muscles to clench him tighter.

"Damn, baby. You know what that does to me," Bryson said, angling her forward and thrusting harder. He lifted her leg higher and plunged deeper, faster until he climaxed.

Another orgasm ripped through Raven and she screamed out his name.

"My sweet Raven. I love you."

Tears burned her eyes. She loved him more than her own life.

Several minutes later, after their breathing slowed, Bryson said, "I guess we should probably shower and go down to breakfast. We don't want to be late for the first day."

She snorted. "Speak for yourself."

He chuckled and patted her on the butt. "Come on. Today is all about exercising and I *know* you're going to have that competitive spirit working."

Raven scooted off the bed. "Yeah, whatever." He was right, however. Out of the four friends, she tended to be the one who kept up an exercise regimen. She chuckled inwardly thinking about Ryleigh. The girl hated working out. Raven headed for the bathroom to shower.

Half an hour later, she and Bryson sat in the Inn's restaurant eating and Raven had to make herself slow down and not devour the large Belgian waffle on her plate in four bites. "Oh, my goodness, this is so good. And it tastes just like I remember."

Bryson smiled and shook his head. "I've got my own and I'm not going to take your food, so you can take your time."

She glared at him. "If somebody hadn't got all...all...you know." She waved a hand. "We would've been down here earlier and I wouldn't have to eat fast."

He leaned forward and a sexy grin spread across his lips. "I take full responsibility and I'll do it again...with *pleasure*."

His low tone and knowing look set off a pulsing in her core and she squeezed her legs together to quell the feeling. Pointing her fork at him, she said, "Eat." He picked up his fork, but the heat in his eyes had her thinking about his earlier statement: *I'm tempted to keep you here all day.* She would gladly stay locked up with him, touching him, kissing him, licking—"

"Raven!"

Raven blinked. "Huh? What? Did you say something?"

Bryson frowned. "I called your name three times. Are you okay? You're not worried about the boot camp, are you?"

She waved him off. "I'm fine and no, I'm not worried." No way would she tell him what she'd been thinking. They'd be back upstairs before the words left her mouth. On second thought, it might not be a bad idea, especially if it meant skipping the whole boot camp nonsense. She sighed and continued eating. These were her girls and she'd given her word.

When they arrived at the camp later, Raven greeted Ryleigh, Quinn, Ava and Mac, then took a seat.

Bryson leaned over and whispered, "Are you ready?"

"As ready as I'm going to be." Raven settled in to listen to the man and woman leading the camp. The guy, who introduced himself as Ricky, reminded her of a Richard Simmons throwback, frizzy hair and all. Philomena, with her bright colors that were nowhere in the vicinity of matching, and we-are-one-with-the-universe aura, reminded Raven of one of the cheerleaders she'd hated in high school. She wanted them to shut up and get to the workout. Both of them were so "cheery" they were giving her a headache. And she had to suffer with them being their personal coaches for the entire four days. *I can't do this.* She glanced over at her friends. Of course, Ava didn't have anything to worry about since she'd popped out two babies already. She was just there for support. Quinn, as usual, was totally focused, Mac had a take it or leave it expression, and Ryleigh looked as if she was going to hurt somebody, and soon. Bryson nudged her.

"Why are you frowning?"

"They. Keep. Talking," she gritted out. "I thought we're

supposed to be working out. And it better not be like one of those damn eighties videos with the woman wearing spandex and leg warmers doing some lame jumping jack and toe touch routine." If that happened, she was out. Promise or not.

Bryson smothered a laugh behind a fake cough.

"It's not funny, Bryse."

"Yeah, girl, it is." He gave her a once over. "Maybe we should go find you an appropriate outfit. I happen to think you'd look pretty sexy in spandex."

Raven glared at him. She wanted to punch him in the chest.

As if reading her thoughts, he leaned close to her ear and whispered, "You remember what happened the last time you punched me in the chest? Yeah, I know that's what you're thinking."

She remembered exactly what happened. The same thing that happened when she'd been teasing him and called his muscles itty bitty. He'd picked her up and tossed her in the air as if she were a bag of chips. Sure, she trusted him and had known that he wouldn't have dropped her, but that wasn't the point. The look on his face dared her to do it. Knowing he'd make good on his threat, she rolled her eyes and tuned back into whatever Philomena was saying. A moment later, Raven felt herself zoning out again and had to force herself to pay attention. She had no idea how she was going to deal with this for the next three days of the healthy eating, Zen whatever and sexuality aspects of the boot camp. In fact, they could completely skip that last day. Bryson had that particular area all wrapped up. "Finally," she muttered when the coaches announced the workout plan.

"You ready, baby?" Bryson stood and helped her up.

"Yeah, babe, especially since there's a prize in the mix." She followed them over to the workout area and went through all the stretches. Because of her crazy schedule over the past couple weeks, Raven hadn't exercised consistently and she was looking forward to a good workout.

After the stretches, they started with a few upper body exercises, including pushups, then moved to the lower body. They rested for two minutes between exercises, double the time she usually did and Raven had a hard time waiting. The fifty lunges had her thighs burning, but she enjoyed it. Having Bryson next to her made it even better. They'd worked out together occasionally over the years and did one-on-one volleyball or basketball games, but even more so since they married. It was their special time to talk, vent, bounce ideas and work through any issues. She looked forward to it almost as much as she did cuddling in bed with him. Glancing over at him doing the squats and seeing the muscles of his thighs flex with each movement, had her contemplating trying to convince him to work out naked. She wasn't sure how much they'd get done, but something would be *worked out*.

"Halfway there," he said.

Raven squatted, making sure she had proper form—butt going back as if sitting in a chair, knees not going past the toes. She checked out her girls. "Come on, sisters. *Push through!* We've got this." That earned her a couple of dirty looks, but she just smiled. The final exercise was a lap around the track, which they could run or walk. She opted to run and, of course, her competitive nature kicked in. Bryson was pretty quick because he'd played basketball in high school and conditioning was part of the program. However, she'd been a sprinter in high school and college. The two-hundred and four-hundred meter races were her specialty. She could run one lap around the track without breathing hard. "If I win, you buy me two dozen butter cookies from Roseberry Bakery."

Bryson folded his arms and cocked his head to the side. "And if I win, I get another round at the tree down by the lake."

She grinned. "Deal." Either way, she'd come out a winner. But she really wanted more of those cookies and didn't plan to lose. Since they'd arrived, Raven had only been able to get three cookies. She was overdue.

"By the way, I don't think two dozen cookies fits with this whole healthy eating thing we're supposed to be embarking on."

"Ask me if I care. I'm getting those cookies and enough to take home and freeze. Let's go." Bryson did the countdown and they took off. They were fairly even for the first two-hundred meters, then he pulled ahead slightly. Raven didn't worry. She let him. When they hit the final curve, she increased her speed, caught him and edged out in front. The last twenty-five meters, she left him in the dust and crossed the finish line. She pumped her fists in the air and did a little hop. "*Yessss!* We're getting those cookies as soon as we leave here."

Bryson bent over at the waist, trying to catch his breath. "Okay, I'll give you this one. And you won the day."

Raven flexed her biceps. "Say my name."

He laughed. "We keep going this way, we'll have this baby challenge in the bag within the next week."

His words gave her pause. She'd momentarily forgotten about the whole pregnancy part. How was she going to tell him that she was afraid? And why.

*M*onday morning, Bryson stared down at the contents of his plate. When they'd gotten home from South Carolina yesterday, he had suggested to Raven that they try a few of the recipes from the boot camp. Seeing the carrot "bacon" and the green concoction in the glass had him wishing he'd kept his mouth shut. His gaze strayed to the blueberry muffins they'd brought back from the bakery, along with Raven's butter cookies. Right now, that muffin sounded like a better option.

"Well?"

"Looks good." True, it did resemble bacon and even had the smoky smell like it, but he decided to work his way up to it and started with the scrambled egg whites, something he actually could eat. Obviously, she'd made the same decision because she picked up the piece of wheat toast and took a bite.

"This would taste so much better with some of my mother's strawberry jam."

"I thought we were going to try to cut out sugar and meat for at least a couple days a week."

"The key word is *try*. And I'm not talking about slathering on the entire jar, just a little. I skipped the butter, so I should be able to have something on this dry bread."

Bryson conceded that point to her. He wasn't too keen on dry toast either. Unlike Raven, who only used a small amount of butter and jam, he *slathered* it on. "Okay, we can add just enough for flavor."

Raven jumped up from the table before the words were out of his mouth good. She came back to the table with one of the four jars her mother had given them and a knife. After spreading a thin layer, she took a bite. "Mmm, this is so good."

He added some to his toast and groaned with the first bite.

"See, I told you. You're not going to want store bought anymore."

"You're right. How much do you think your mom would charge to have a steady shipment every three months?"

She laughed. "For you, nothing. I can't believe she still does all that giggling and blushing every time we go home."

"Don't hate." From the moment the older woman had found out he and Raven were dating, she'd started showering him with love, food, and any other thing he wanted. She hadn't stopped.

She rolled her eyes and ate a bite of eggs.

Bryson finished everything except the "bacon." Taking a deep breath, he picked up a piece and took a bite. He frowned and tried to erase the taste from his mouth. This was *not* bacon and he was torn between swallowing and spitting it out. He snatched up the glass of green smoothie and took a big sip, hoping it would help. He pushed his chair back so fast it tipped over and made a mad dash to the kitchen sink where he spit it all out. "*Ugh!* What the hell is in this?" He coughed and coughed, then snatched the refrigerator open and grabbed the carton of orange juice. Not bothering with a glass, he took a huge swig. It didn't help.

"That bad?" Raven asked, laughing so hard she had tears in her eyes.

"*Worse.*" He tilted the carton to his mouth again.

"Well, I'm going to take your word for the carrots. The smoothie isn't too bad once you get used to the green taste. There's spinach, kale, peaches, pineapples, apples and flaxseed." She picked up her plate, walked over and dumped the carrots into the garbage disposal.

He didn't agree, but kept it to himself since he was supposed to be supportive. "I'm heading out so I can go see if Jerome still has my center standing." He and his best friend and business partner, Jerome Smith, had started Impressions Community Center five years ago after Bryson left his job as an inpatient clinical psychologist. He'd always loved kids and wanted to make a difference in their lives, and give them a place where they could find support if they had problems. The suicide of his college girlfriend had played a small part in his decision. He couldn't help her, but he could make sure it didn't happen again to some other young person.

Raven smiled. "Jerome is just as anal as you, so you know nothing's going to be out of place. Is Ken still volunteering to teach during the summer program this year with his wedding coming up?"

"He said he'd still do the first couple of weeks, but recommended another one of his colleagues to finish out the session." Kendrick Johnson rounded out the quartet who had all been best friends since college. Bryson smiled at the memory of Jerome and Kendrick's reaction when Bryson and Raven started dating. They had been just as shocked as he and Raven by the sudden feelings and they'd threatened to kill him if he broke her heart. Once they realized he was very serious about Raven, they got on board. Bryson never had a problem with him and Raven making the transition from best friends to lovers, and to forever partners because he loved her with every fiber of his being. And breaking her heart would mean breaking his own and he had no intentions of that ever happening. "Do you have a long day?"

"If all the PTs are there, I shouldn't. But I have a couple of new athletes to evaluate at the end of the day and it may take longer. Hopefully, I'll make it home around five, since I'm doing the early shift."

"I'll start dinner if I get home first." Whatever he cooked would include real meat.

"Okay." Raven came up on her tiptoes and kissed him. "I'll see you tonight."

Bryson knew he should end the kiss. He had a long day ahead of him. But he'd never been able to resist her kisses. He groaned when she slid her hands over his chest, abdomen and quickly rising erection. He broke off the kiss. "Stop that. You're going to make me late."

"Just giving you a little taste of your own medicine. Remember last week when you made me have to rush my waffles?" She tossed him a wink and strutted out of the room.

He laughed and called out, "I didn't hear you complaining and we went back again." Shaking his head, he picked up his bag and started for the garage. As he passed the counter, he paused and glanced over his shoulder to make sure Raven had gone upstairs. When he didn't hear anything, he eased the top off the container holding the muffins and took the biggest one. After securing the container once again, Bryson dropped his muffin into a Ziploc bag and, smiling, headed out.

When Bryson arrived at the center he found Jerome seated in his office reading over some papers. "It's good to see the center still standing."

Jerome's head came up. "Well if it isn't the slacker. About time you brought your ass back to work."

He entered and took the chair across from Jerome's desk. "If you found a woman to settle down with, you could see the outside of this office sometimes, too. Trust me, you'd enjoy it." Bryson used to be just as bad about working late hours, but changed his ways as soon as he and Raven got together. She'd helped him learn balance.

"How did things go?" he asked, ignoring Bryson's statement.

Bryson smiled knowingly. With Jerome about to be the only single one in their group, Bryson and Kendrick had begun teasing him about his bachelorhood. "It went well."

Jerome studied Bryson. "That well? You were able to get Raven away from her friends long enough to hang out?"

He stretched out his long legs and leaned back in the chair. "Actually, we ended up spending time with the whole crew, husbands included. Remember when I told you that Raven and her girls always made those Best Friends Challenges?"

"Like the marriage-in-a-year one?"

He nodded. "This time the challenge is for them all to become pregnant within a year."

Jerome's mouth fell open. "Are you kidding me? And Raven agreed?"

"I think, like the last one, this one was all Quinn again. The woman is a diehard romantic and she got them all to participate in a four-day session at Baby Bump Boot Camp."

He burst out laughing. "Baby bump what?" He shook his head and held up a hand. "Okay, wait. So there's a camp that's supposed to help you get pregnant?"

Bryson chuckled. "No. It's all about helping participants prepare themselves before, during and after. You know, exercise, healthy eating, relaxation and, my personal favorite, sexuality."

"Yeah, I'm sure that's no hardship. And Raven?"

"She hasn't said much, but you know she was all in on the workout day." He didn't share with Jerome the mixed feelings he'd been sensing from her. One minute she seemed fine and the next, not so much. But when he had asked about it, she said she was good. This would definitely be a big change in their lives, and they had discussed and agreed that they wanted children. So he would take her at her word. For now. Changing the subject, he asked, "Is Ken coming in today?"

"Yep. Said he'd get here around ten because it was summer and he wasn't punching the clock at six in the morning until he had to." Kendrick taught high school calculus.

"I can't blame him. I miss the days of sleeping in." Bryson stood.

"Well you'd better stock up now because it sounds like your days are going to be filled with two a.m. feedings and diaper changes in the near future."

"Maybe, but I don't mind. I'd better get started whittling down my email inbox. See you later."

In his office, while waiting for his computer to load, he broke off a piece of the muffin and popped it in his mouth. He groaned. Now *this* was food. He took a sip of his coffee. Even still, it didn't erase the foul taste of smoked, burnt carrots, dirt, and grass. Just the thought turned his stomach. Yeah, he was chucking their originally planned dinner menu in favor of *real* food.

~

"Hallelujah, you're back!"

Raven laughed at her coworker and locked her purse in

her desk drawer. "David, I've only been gone for *one* week. You act like it's been months." She raised a brow. "Did something happen while I was gone?"

"Nothing other than we were one or two therapists down just about every day. John had something with his kids and Eileen has been out sick since Wednesday. With any luck, she'll be in today. She hasn't called in yet, so I'm keeping my fingers crossed."

"I hope so." Raven didn't want to have to deal with the extra paperwork on her first day back. After stashing her lunch in the break room refrigerator, she booted up her computer and checked her schedule. Other than the two new patients, her existing clients were well set on their programs and she should be able to breeze through the day.

Thankfully, Eileen had come in, which meant Raven could sit and eat her lunch without rushing. After the disastrous breakfast, she'd made herself a turkey sandwich on a French roll with lettuce, tomatoes, pickles and honey mustard, and stopped at the mini mart near the office for chips. She had noticed a blueberry muffin missing and had to laugh because Bryson had read her mind. She'd done the same and the delectable taste had more than made up for that that carrot masquerading as bacon. In her mind, nothing could take the place of the salty, smoky meat. Quinn, Mac, Ava, and Ryleigh didn't need to know she planned to keep her seventy-five percent healthy eating plan, bacon, *and* her butter cookies. She'd brought back four dozen for herself and one for Bryson because, as much as she loved her husband, she did *not* share her cookies with anyone.

Raven finished her sandwich and chips, then excitedly reached for the bag holding her three cookies. She had purposely scheduled herself for the late lunch so she could have the breakroom to herself. Biting into the first one, she nearly swooned in her chair. "Mmm." Raven closed her eyes and savored the experience—rich, buttery, slightly sweet and full of *have mercy* goodness. Mrs. Oak's famous recipe had soothed her on many occasions and today was no exception.

"Are those butter cookies?"

She slowly opened her eyes and stared at Eileen. The woman had no idea how dangerously close she was to Raven channeling a Mac cuss-out. However, Raven figured that wouldn't go over too well and kept the litany of colorful words to herself. "Yes."

"Ooh, those are my favorites, and those are much larger than the ones I've seen in the stores. They must be homemade."

"Mine, too. And they're pretty close to homemade." Eileen stood there as if waiting for Raven to offer her one. Not a day went by when the woman didn't try to beg one of the staff out of their food. *If she's waiting for one of these cookies, she'll be waiting until hell freezes over.* Raven took another bite and made a show of searching through the emails on her cell. Finally, Eileen took the hint and left. Raven chuckled and went back to her cookies, smiling and humming.

As soon as she finished, her cell chimed. She read the text from her cousin, Erika, wanting to know about the trip. Raven glanced at her watch. Her next patient would be there in less than five minutes, so Raven sent a quick reply to let her cousin know she'd call her that evening on the way home. She disposed of her trash, drank the rest of her water and headed back to the treatment area.

The rest of the afternoon went by in a blur and she was more than ready to leave at closing time.

"Hey, Raven. Since you weren't sharing your cookies earlier, can you at least tell me where you got them so I can stop on my way home," Eileen said, lounging in the doorway with her purse slung over her shoulder.

Raven laughed. "You'll be driving a long time. I brought them back from South Carolina."

"Are you serious?"

"Yep." She packed up and retrieved her purse. "The bakery has been there since I was a kid and the cookies haven't changed in all that time."

Eileen sighed and threw up her hands. "Why is it every time I see something good, it's doggone near impossible to get?"

"I have no idea."

She shot Raven a glare as they walked out to the parking lot. "Now I'm going to have to find a good recipe."

Raven smiled. "Let me know how it goes. See you tomorrow." They parted ways and she slid in behind the wheel, started the engine and connected her phone to the Bluetooth so she could call Erika back.

"Hey, Doc. How did the trip go?"

Shaking her head at the doctor reference, she merged onto the street. "It was good to see my crazy friends again and Baby Sully is adorable. I couldn't believe how much Maddie has grown. Mom and Dad are good. They're planning a getaway to the Caribbean soon."

"Aw, that's so cute. I need to hurry up and be grown enough to just take off to some country whenever I feel like it."

"Girl, me, too. But we've got a good twenty years before then." Raven's father still worked as the town's physician, although he'd begun to cut back on his hours and take more time off. Her mother had retired after more than twenty-five years as a nurse practitioner.

"No lie, but I can dream. So the crew is all good? No other babies?"

"They're all good and no babies, although if Quinn had

her way, we'd all have at least two by now. She roped us into another pact."

Erika chuckled. "A baby pact?"

"Sort of. We're all supposed to get pregnant in a year or we have to pay for the next girls trip." Seeing the freeway traffic, Raven decided to take the surface streets.

"Ha! You'd better hurry up because I know y'all won't be going anywhere cheap."

"That's a guarantee." She thought about confiding in Erika about her fears surrounding motherhood, but she was only five minutes from home and it would take longer than that. She also didn't want Bryson to hear it. Raven directed the conversation toward Erika and her husband. They spent the remainder of the time catching up.

"Are you guys doing anything for the Fourth next month?"

"I don't know yet. For the past couple of years, we've been hanging out with Kendrick and Jerome. I'll find out whether they're planning to do the same and let you know." Raven heard a deep voice, then muffled giggling. "I guess your hubby is home."

"You guessed right," Erika said in a voice that told Raven exactly what that giggling had been about.

"Tell Vance I said hello. We need to do lunch soon." Erika had always filled the role of the older sister Raven never had.

"I'll text you tomorrow with a couple of dates and times. Most likely it'll need to be on a weekend. I've been leaving the hospital late more often than not." Erika worked as a nurse manager.

"That works. Talk to you later." She disconnected and pulled into her driveway a few minutes later. She opened the garage and saw Bryson's car. She wondered what he was cooking for dinner and secretly prayed it had nothing to do with any of the recipes Philomena had given them. Inside, the fragrance of sautéed peppers and onions hit her nose. Her stomach growled. "Please tell me whatever is going with those peppers is edible and includes regular food and I'll love you forever."

Bryson turned and sent a smile her way. "If that's the only reason you're planning to love me forever, it's going to be more of that fake bacon."

She gave him a sensual smile, sauntered over to where he stood at the counter and slid her arms around his waist. "Baby, you know I'm going to love you forever anyway because you are my heart." She couldn't imagine loving anyone else or going through this thing called life without him.

He pressed a sweet, lingering kiss to her forehead. "And you're mine. We're having chicken fajitas. Does that get me closer to that forever?"

Raven wrapped her arms around her neck and pulled his head down into a deep kiss. She swirled her tongue around his, infusing it with all the love she felt for him. At length, she eased back. "Does that answer your question?"

Bryson smiled. "For now. I might have a few more questions later, though. You can help me answer them and then we can see about being first in the challenge."

Just like that, her stomach dropped. She smiled, but inside, she thought about maybe losing and wondered whether she should start saving money for that girls trip.

CHAPTER 2

*T*he following Monday afternoon, Bryson sat in his office staring out the window. He had a ton of things he should be doing, but his mind was on Raven. They'd been back from South Carolina a week and he still couldn't dismiss the sensation that something was up with her. It wasn't anything she'd said or done, just a strong feeling. He'd known her since she was eighteen and could read her moods well. He also knew that she had a tendency to shut down when she became overwhelmed. Thinking back, the shift seemed to have occurred right after she told him about the pact. Had she changed her mind about wanting children? His heart clenched. Bryson sat straight up. He'd always wanted at least two kids because, as an only child, loneliness had been his companion many times and he didn't want any children he had to experience the same.

"Knock, knock. Can I come in?"

He rotated his chair toward the door where his administrative assistant, Tonya Franklin stood. "Hey, Tonya. Have a seat. Let me call Jerome and we can talk." He lifted the receiver and pushed the intercom. When Jerome answered, Bryson let him know Tonya was here for their meeting.

Tonya stared at him curiously and sat in one of the chairs across from Bryson's desk. "What's going on, Bryson?"

Bryson smiled. "Relax, Tonya. It's nothing bad."

"Okay," she said skeptically.

Jerome entered and closed the door. "Hey, Tonya." He took the seat next to her.

Bryson clasped his hands together on the desk and leaned forward. "Tonya, we know that you've been working hard for the past two years dividing your time between getting everything ready for the new preschool and keeping up with all your other administrative duties and you've gone above and beyond our expectations." He had hired Tonya Franklin shortly after opening the center. Following back surgery, the forty-something-year-old woman couldn't return to her former position as a preschool teacher because of the physical nature of the job.

"I appreciate you trusting me to get it done. It's been hard work, but I've enjoyed every moment and can't wait until it opens next month. We've gotten at least forty applications already and you're going to need to hire someone to direct the program."

Bryson and Jerome shared a smile. "I already have. You."

Her eyes widened and she divided a stunned gaze between Bryson and Jerome. "Are you kidding me?"

"No," Jerome said. "Who better to head the program than the woman who almost singlehandedly put it together."

Bryson handed her a sheet of paper. "This would be your new salary."

Tonya read for a moment before letting out a loud, *"Yes!"* She clapped a hand over her mouth. "Sorry."

Jerome laughed and waved her off. "Does that mean you'll take the job?"

"You'd better believe it." She paused. "What about my old position? Who's going to keep you two in line?"

Bryson chuckled. "We'll put out an ad, unless you have a recommendation."

"Give me a day or so to think about it. And don't worry, it'll be someone who can live up to your exacting standards."

"I don't know what you mean," he said with feigned innocence. Bryson was anal to a fault about his business and she knew it.

"Mmm hmm," Tonya said with a smile. Then she turned serious. "Thank you both so much for trusting me with this. It's going to be the best preschool in the state."

"I have no doubts about that."

"By the way, there are still a few more things we need to purchase and I scheduled the teacher interviews for later this week and all of next week. I'll have the list to you no later than tomorrow. I want to be sure I haven't missed anything." She stood.

Bryson and Jerome followed suit and Bryson said, "That's fine." He waited until she left before turning to Jerome. "Well, what do you think?"

"I think we're smart as hell for promoting her. She's shared some of what she has planned and she's right. It just might be the best program in the state. Oh, and that suggestion from Raven about hiring students as teacher assistants is saving us money, as well. Speaking of Raven, how are things going with the latest challenge? Pregnant yet?"

"No, but we've been getting some good practice." He glanced down at his watch. "And I'm cutting out early to see if we can do another session."

Jerome made a face and held up a hand. "Stop. Just stop. It's hard enough thinking about you and Raven being more than friends, so I don't need to know all those intimate details."

Bryson laughed. "Yeah, well. What can I say?"

"Nothing. Don't say another word."

Kendrick poked his head in the door. "Am I the only one here working today? There's way too much laughing and goofing off going on in this office."

"I was just telling Rome about me doing my part to help Raven and I be the first to win the challenge."

He frowned. "I don't even want to know. Raven is like my sister and that's just TMI, man."

Jerome gestured toward Kendrick, "See, that's what I'm talking about."

Still chuckling, Bryson said, "Oh, before I forget, are we doing the barbeque for the Fourth again?"

"Hadn't really thought about it, but it's only a couple of weeks away, so we'd better decide. Isn't it your turn to host?"

"I think so." They usually rotated between his, Jerome's and Kendrick's houses.

"Oh, then I'm definitely in," Kendrick and Jerome said at the same time.

"I bet. We can get a menu together later this week. Right now, I'm packing up and going home to my beautiful wife." Bryson turned off his computer and straightened the folders on his desk.

Kendrick nodded. "I'm looking forward to doing the same." He would be getting married in three weeks.

Bryson and Kendrick stared at Jerome.

Jerome snorted. "Don't look at me. I keep telling y'all I like my bachelorhood."

"Forty is right around the corner, my brother," Kendrick said, clapping Jerome on the shoulder, "and as I said before, leaning on a cane when you drop your kid off for kindergarten is *not* a good look."

Bryson howled with laughter.

Jerome threw up the finger and stalked out.

"I hope he figures out having that one special woman is better than anything in this world. It took me a couple of tries to get it right, but I know Joelle is my one and only." Kendrick had been previously engaged, but broke it off when he found out the woman had cheated on him.

"I agree. How are the wedding plans going?" Bryson asked as they left his office.

"Everything is pretty much taken care of, aside from a few things, like food for the rehearsal dinner and the gifts for the wedding party."

"Let me know if you need me to do anything." He and Jerome were standing in as best men.

"I will. I'm going to finish up with the last of the curriculum and head out. Tell Raven hi and text me with what you want me to bring for the barbeque."

"Okay. See you tomorrow." He rounded the corner and called out a goodbye to Tonya as he passed her desk, making a mental note to clear out one of the unused offices for her to use. Not for the first time, he was grateful that he and Jerome had the foresight to lease a building that allowed them to expand in response to the community's growing needs.

Traffic turned out to be much heavier than he expected for four-thirty in the afternoon and it took him double the time to get home. He smiled when he saw Raven's car parked in the garage. Bryson entered through the kitchen and found her standing at the sink rinsing an apple. She had already changed out of her work attire into shorts and a T-shirt. His gaze traveled down to her bare feet. She had always preferred dressing comfortably.

"Hey, baby." He pressed a kiss to her temple.

"Hey. You're home early."

"Yep." He wiggled his eyebrows. "I figured we could get started a little early." He nuzzled her neck and slid his hands beneath her shirt. Raven ducked out of his embrace and he frowned. "What's wrong?" He closed the distance between them and pulled her into his embrace. "Talk to me, sweetheart."

"Nothing. It's just..." Raven sighed and set the apple on the counter. "It just seems like every time we...we...have sex, it's all about trying to make a baby."

Bryson went still.

"Don't get me wrong, the sex is good, I mean great, but lately, it feels so, so, *functional*. I miss us just being in bed together without an agenda."

He'd never thought about it from that perspective, but she was right. Each time had been about him trying to win the prize. He sighed and held her closer. "I'm sorry, and you're right. That's not how I want it to be between us." Bryson tilted her chin and stared at the woman who had captured every corner of his heart. He brushed a kiss over her lips. "How about we forget about the challenge and go back to the way things were. If it happens it does. No pressure." He took her hand and led her out to the swing he'd had built on the patio as a wedding gift. It was similar to the one her parents had and she'd once confided that sitting with him made her feel safe and he never wanted her to be without that sense of security. Once seated, he wrapped his arm around Raven's shoulder and set the swing to a slow sway.

Raven laid her head on his shoulder. "Thanks, Bryse."

They didn't talk, just sat in quiet companionship, yet Bryson knew there was more going on with her than what she'd told him. He hoped they would be able to work through whatever it turned out to be.

Raven basked in the contentment she felt sitting with Bryson. The whole baby challenge had her so unsure of herself she didn't know whether she was coming or going. She wondered if Mac, Ryleigh and Quinn were feeling the same kind of pressure and made a mental note to check in with them soon. The lulling motion of the swing relaxed her and she found herself dozing off.

"Raven?"

She startled slightly. "Hmm."

"Ken and Rome wanted to know if we're doing the barbeque around the Fourth again this year."

"I'm good with that. I'll see if Simeon wants to come, too." Her attorney brother worked more hours than was healthy and, like most protective big sisters, she worried about him burning out.

"I'll let them know." After a couple of minutes, Bryson asked, "Are you ready to tell me what's really bothering you? I know it's more than the sex. I can sense it."

Raven had hoped he wouldn't ask because, yes, there was more than the sex, and no, she wasn't ready. She didn't know how to tell him everything swirling around in her mind. She closed her eyes and tried to choose her words.

"Did you change your mind about us having kids?"

Raven could hear the uncertainty in his voice. She could recall several times over the years when they'd shared their dreams that children had always been part of the plan. Until that night. "I'm not sure," she said after a lengthy pause, staring out into the yard. She avoided looking his way because she couldn't stand to see the hurt in his eyes, the fear that they were no longer on the same page. But he took the decision out of her hands when he pulled her onto his lap.

"Are you saying you don't want them anymore? We talked about this a lot and you never mentioned changing your mind. Why now?"

When she didn't answer, he repeated the question. It took all she had to force the words past her lips. "Because I'm scared. I'm afraid that I don't have what it takes to be a mother."

Bryson caressed her cheek. "Baby, you're going to be a fantastic mother."

"But what if I'm not?"

He scrutinized her a long moment. "Where is this coming from, Raven? You've never been this worried about having a baby, or anything else for that matter. In fact, you're the one who always tackles a problem head on."

That much was true. Not much scared her, and when something did, Raven went full force with the determination of a warrior. She had run away from one thing only—her love for him. But he never gave up on her or them. Now, she was running again.

"Whatever it is, we'll deal with it together. Tell me what has you so afraid."

The plea in his eyes made her heart clench. Taking a deep breath, she said, "Darren."

Bryson's expression went from concerned to angry in a blink of the eye. "Darren? What did he say to you?"

Raven blew out a long breath. "He'd been hinting around at us taking our relationship to the next level and I asked him whether he wanted kids." She would never forget his incredulous expression or his harsh laughter. "He said absolutely not. That he didn't want to be burdened with that kind of long-term expense. Then he told me..." A lump formed in her throat. "He told me he hoped I hadn't considered motherhood because a kid would be better off going through the system than having me for a mother. He tried to laugh it off afterward and say he'd been kidding and that he just meant that I was so career focused he couldn't see me putting my job on hold for a child. I wanted to believe him, so I let it pass. Then, a couple of weeks later, the whole blow-up over dinner happened." On that night, she happened to see two of her physical therapy clients at the restaurant where she and her ex were having dinner. He accused her of being too "cozy" and wanted her to change jobs because he was insecure about the male athletes who came to the rehab clinic. They got into it, Raven ended the relationship and ended up taking a cab home when he left her stranded.

Bryson jumped up, ran a hand over his shoulder-length locs and paced in front of her.

"Until then, outside of the normal doubts, I wasn't too worried about whether I'd be a good mother. I tried not to give his words any credence and had buried them in my mind."

He stopped pacing. "Until you made the pact with your friends."

"Yes." She waited for him to say something else, but he just stood there with his jaw clenched and his chest heaving. Was he angry because she hadn't told him earlier?

Finally, he came back to the swing. Bryson cradled her face between his large hands. "Listen to me, Raven, nothing he said is true." He rested his forehead against hers and closed his eyes, as if trying to maintain control. "Not one word of it," he gritted out.

Raven could feel his body trembling. "I keep trying to tell myself that, but, somewhere deep inside me, I wonder. What if I do something wrong?"

"You won't do anything wrong, sweetheart. I *know* you. Who are you going to believe—a self-serving asshole or the man who adores you, the one who'd give his life for you and who has your back no matter what?"

His passionate words filled her with emotions so strong they nearly overwhelmed her. She tried to keep the tears from falling, but failed. *Dammit! I hate crying.* "You, Bryson. I believe you."

He kissed her softly, wiped away her tears and stood. "I need to leave for a bit, okay?"

She scrambled off the swing in a panic. "Where are you going?"

Bryson scrubbed a hand down his face. "I don't know. I just have to go."

"Are you angry with me?" Her heart pounded as she waited for his response.

"I'm mad as hell right now, but not at you. All my anger is directed at the man who put that fear inside you, and it's a good thing he's not around. If he was, I'd kick his ass."

Raven knew he would make good on that threat. He'd put the fear of God into at least two of her past boyfriends in college when they stepped out of line with her and it had taken a Herculean effort on her part to convince him not to beat them to a pulp. This time his anger felt different, more intense and it concerned her.

"I promise I won't be gone long."

She nodded and watched him stride into the kitchen, snatch his keys off the hook and rush out the door. She slowly lowered herself onto the swing. One part of her was glad she'd finally shared her fears with him. The other part felt like she had exchanged one fear for another. Bryson had said his anger wasn't directed at her, but she saw the pain reflected in his face and it scared her to think things might change between them. *He's not like that*, an inner voice chimed. She wrapped her arms around herself and prayed she was right. Her stomach growled and she went inside for the apple she'd left on the counter. She picked it up, intending to take a bite, but her nerves were so bad, she put it back down.

Raven wouldn't be okay until Bryson came back. She tried to distract herself with the television and music, but nothing worked. Time seemed to pass slowly and her anxiety mounted with each passing second. When she finally heard the garage door opening after almost an hour, she nearly sprinted out the door to meet him. Bryson climbed out of the car and she launched herself into his arms. "Are you okay?"

"I'm better."

"And now that you're home, so am I."

He held up a bag. "I figured I'd pick something up for dinner."

She grinned. "Is that a cheeseburger I smell?"

"Yep. And French fries."

"I love you so much, and after I'm done with my burger, I'm going to show you how much." She tossed him a wink.

Bryson laughed.

He always did know how to make her feel better.

CHAPTER 3

*B*ryson stood at the sink seasoning the ribs. Because of everyone's schedule, they'd decided to hold their gathering on the weekend following the Fourth of July holiday, instead. He shifted slightly and watched Raven peel potatoes while she danced to the music flowing from the portable speaker. Since she'd shared the root of her fears about having a baby, she'd been more relaxed and like her old self. His anger rose all over again when he thought about what her ex had said. Bryson considered himself to be relatively even tempered. However, that day, he wanted to find Darren and whip his ass. Bryson couldn't remember the last time he had been so angry, which was why he'd had to leave the house for a while. He'd been a heartbeat away from losing control and he didn't want Raven to see him that way. After he came home they'd talked, cuddled on the swing and he'd held her all night long. Since then, even their love-making had been different, more intimate and tied to nothing but passion. He smiled as she continued to shake her hips in time with the beat.

"Are you going to stand there staring at me all day? Everybody will be here in an hour."

He blinked and met her amused expression. *Busted.* "If you weren't over there trying to tempt me with all that hip motion, I could get something done."

Raven gave him a sultry smile, then did an exaggerated hip sway, complete with a dip. "You mean when I drop it like it's hot like this?"

"Don't make me cancel this get together."

She laughed. "Sorry, it's too late for that. Besides, there's way too much food and we can't let it go to waste."

Bryson started toward her and the doorbell rang.

"Saved by the bell," she said with a chuckle.

"Lucky you." Bryson washed his hands and went to answer the door, muttering about his tease of a wife. Raven's brother stood there with two bags in his hands. "Hey, Simeon."

"What's up, Bryse?" Simeon said, entering and going straight to the kitchen. He placed the bags on the counter and kissed Raven on the cheek. "Hey, sis."

"Hey, yourself. You look tired."

He smiled. "You know the drill—work, work, work."

Raven frowned. "You need to slow down. How many times have I told you that working yourself to death will only—"

"Ah, babe, your brother is a grown man and I'm sure he can manage his life just fine," Bryson cut in.

"Of course, you'd take his side. You men are all alike." She rolled her eyes and went back to dicing the potatoes.

Bryson and Simeon shared a look and Simeon mouthed, "That's *your* wife." Aloud he said, "What do you need me to do?"

Bryson put him to work, finished putting the dry rub on the ribs, then went to start the grill. Twenty minutes later,

Jerome, Kendrick and Kendrick's fiancée, Joelle arrived. While the women worked in the kitchen, the men stood around outside drinking beers, laughing and talking. Jerome and Bryson took turns manning the grill.

"You know who called me last night?" Kendrick said.

Bryson paused in turning the meat. "Who?"

"Sandra."

Jerome choked on his beer. "What did she want?"

"She apologized for cheating on me again, said she'd made a mistake and wants us to try again," he added with a snort. "She actually had the nerve to say that she'd given me plenty of time to get over the incident, as if that should make a difference."

"I hope you set her straight," Bryson said.

"Oh, I did. Told her I was over the incident...*and* her."

They all roared with laughter.

"Where do you all find these women?" Simeon asked, shaking his head. "I assume that was the end of the conversation."

"You assume wrong. She figured since I let her keep the engagement ring, that meant something. It did. It meant that I didn't want to go through the hassle of selling it back," Kendrick added.

"Good for you, Ken. And every time she looks at it, she's gets a reminder of how stupid she was for messing up a good thing," Raven said, handing a tray of teriyaki chicken to Bryson for him to add to the grill. She kissed Kendrick's cheek. "Crazy heffa. Oh, and I really like Joelle. Can't wait for you guys to get married, so I can have someone local to hang out with that doesn't have a lot of testosterone." She smiled sweetly and went back inside.

"Does anybody else feel like we were dissed and complimented all at the same time?" Jerome asked.

Bryson nodded. "Yeah, that's exactly what it felt like."

Some things stayed the same, and he wouldn't change his wife's smart mouth for all the money in the world. There was never a dull moment with her.

They laughed and continued their conversation. Once all the food was ready, they sat around the table discussing everything from sports to politics. Then the subject of Kendrick and Joelle's wedding came up.

"Are you guys ready for next weekend?" Raven asked.

Joelle smiled at Kendrick. "I've been ready. And I'm even more ready for those two weeks in St. Lucia."

"I bet you are," Bryson said. "Ken, since you're spending a lot of money, you should try to see at least one thing while you're there."

Kendrick let out a short bark of laughter. "As if you and Raven saw more than five minutes outside your hotel room in Barbados."

He couldn't deny that truth. During their honeymoon, he and Raven were content to go from their balcony to the beach, and back to the room. And he was far more interested seeing her in all the sexy lingerie she'd purchased. One particular item stood out in his mind. The skimpy black—" A bump on his shoulder brought him out of his lustful thoughts. "What?"

"Looks like you were taking a trip down memory lane."

Bryson met the smiling faces of his friends. He couldn't deny that, either. "Well, when it's good..." He shrugged and went back to his food.

A short while later, Bryson, Jerome, Kendrick and Simeon played a two-on-two basketball game on the half court at the far end of the yard. They paused for a moment and out of the corner of his eye, Bryson saw Raven leaning against the deck railing with her head bowed. Before he could say anything, she crumpled to the ground. "Raven!" His heart nearly stopped and he sprinted towards the deck, with all the guys on his heels. He dropped to his knees and caressed her cheek. "Raven, baby."

Raven slowly opened her eyes and met Bryson's worried gaze. Then she noticed everyone else hovering over her wearing the same concerned expression.

"Baby, are you okay?"

She tried to figure out what had happened. One minute she was talking to Joelle and the next, she a wave of dizziness like nothing she had ever experienced hit her. *Why am I on the ground?* She sat up. "I'm fine. Just got a little dizzy, that's all." She made a move to stand and Bryson scooped her up in his arms and carried her to the sliding glass door.

"Simeon, can you open the door?" Bryson asked.

Simeon rushed over and complied, his gaze never leaving Raven's.

"You can put me down, Bryse. I'm fine," Raven said as he entered the kitchen.

"You're not fine. If you were, you wouldn't have passed out on the deck." He kept going until they reached the family room where he gently placed her on the sofa.

She blew out a long breath. "Like I said, I just got a little lightheaded for a minute. I'm good now."

"I'm taking you to emergency."

Her eyes widened. "Bryson, I do not need to waste three hours or more in an emergency room for nothing." She searched the gazes of everyone standing around, hoping to find an ally, but all she got were murmurs of agreement.

"I think that's a good idea," Jerome said. "We need to know what happened."

"Seriously, Rome. I'm *fine*."

"Can I have a few minute with my sister, please?" Simeon

directed the question to Bryson, but his gaze remained locked on Raven.

Raven could tell Bryson didn't want to leave, but he finally nodded. Everyone left, reluctantly.

Simeon lowered himself on the sofa next to Raven and took her hand. "Sis, you damn near gave me a heart attack."

"I'm sorry, but I'm okay. Really."

He shook his head slowly. "Maybe, but what if there's something wrong? You need to know why this happened. *I* need to know why. Help your baby brother out and go to the hospital. Please."

She hated when he begged because she caved every. single. time.

"*Please*, Raven."

His emotional plea did her in. "Okay, fine. But I'm telling you, if this takes more than a couple of hours, I'm leaving."

He chuckled. "Deal. As much as I want to tag along, I'm sure my brother-in-law will want to handle this himself."

She rolled her eyes, stood and went to the kitchen. Every eye turned her way. "Fine. Let's go."

Bryson visibly relaxed. "You guys can all stay here. If it's going to be a long wait, I'll text you."

"If it's going to be a long wait, I'm coming back home," Raven countered.

"You are one stubborn woman," Bryson said, gesturing her out the door.

"Like you can talk." She got into the car and closed the door.

He slid behind the wheel and sat for a moment. "You scared the hell out of me, Raven. When I saw you fall like that..." He leaned his head against the steering wheel.

She ran a comforting hand down his back. "I know, and that's the only reason I'm doing this. I don't want you to be worried."

"Thank you," he whispered and started the engine.

They didn't talk on the way, which was just fine for Raven. Truth be told, waking up on the ground had freaked her out a little, especially since she couldn't think of one reason why she'd fainted—no headaches, her blood pressure was normal and she hadn't been sick in forever. When they arrived, they'd found only a few people in the emergency room. *Good. I don't have to be here all day.* Bryson gave her name and the receptionist handed Raven a clipboard with several sheets of paper to fill out and a pen. After finding seats, she started in on the stack. One more thing she hated about coming to the hospital or seeing a new doctor. By the time she finished the only things they hadn't asked were the color of her underwear, where she went to preschool and how many stars she got on her kindergarten homework.

"How are you feeling?"

"I'm good, Bryse." Raven smiled and gave his hand a reassuring squeeze. It took forty-five minutes for her to be called back and the doctor asked just about every question that had been on the forms. When he stepped out, she looked up at Bryson. "I don't know why they had me fill out all that stuff if he was just going to ask me the same stupid questions again."

Bryson smiled. "Maybe they're just being thorough."

She lifted a brow. "Maybe these doctors need to read more." A nurse came in to draw blood and left again.

"I hope there's nothing wrong."

So did she. It seemed like forever before the doctor came in again.

The man smiled. "Congratulations. You're going to be parents."

Good thing Raven was already lying down or she would have fainted again. "*Excuse me.*"

"You're pregnant, Mrs. Montgomery. Most likely, the

fainting was caused by the rise in your hormones." He flipped through the stack of forms she'd completed. "I see that you indicated some past issues with fibroids. I'm going to send you over to the imaging department for an ultrasound to make sure everything is as it should be." He handed her a referral sheet, smiled and slipped out again.

She could not be pregnant. *How in the world did that happen?* Okay, dumb question, but...this wasn't supposed to happen *now*. They'd just made the pact last month. She went still. That meant she had already been pregnant. Raven glanced up at Bryson, whose smile was wide enough to see all thirty-two of his teeth. "I take it you're happy."

"How can you tell?"

Raven shook her head. "Oh, I don't know. Maybe it was the sparkle in your eyes, or that big smile that's bright enough to power every instrument in this hospital." She slid off the gurney. "I guess we should go do this ultrasound."

Still grinning, Bryson followed her out.

It took another hour to get the ultrasound. Raven was surprised to find out that this wouldn't be the normal abdominal one, but transvaginal. *Great.* She laid on the table.

"Okay, Mrs. Montgomery. Let's get started." The woman inserted the probe and moved it around. "We're going to do some measurements and get a more accurate due date." A moment later, she said, "Hmm, interesting."

"Is something wrong?" Bryson asked with concern.

"No, but you might want to take a look at this." She pointed. "This is your baby right here. Here's the head and limb buds. In a few weeks, he or she will have all the body parts."

He stroked Raven's cheek. "Amazing."

"And this is baby number two."

"*What?*" Raven and Bryson said simultaneously.

The ultrasound tech smiled. "You're having twins." She

went on to explain that it was considered a dichorionic pregnancy—the babies came from separate eggs— and said that both heart rates were just over one hundred beats per minute.

"They're strong, rhythmic and steady. Just what we want to see."

Raven merely stared at the screen. She wished she hadn't passed out before finishing her cocktail because she really needed it now. *Twins? Two babies at the same time?* So much for that money she'd started setting aside to pay for the girls trip. *I guess now it'll be going towards a nursery. For two.*

CHAPTER 4

*B*ryson hadn't stopped smiling since finding out he was going to be a father. They'd gone home and made the announcement to their friends and he endured good-natured teasing about his sperm chasing down two eggs. Of course, that knowledge made him stick out his chest a little further. It occurred to him that it might have happened the weekend of the camping trip when he and Raven had a late-night quickie by the lake. The night she'd made him have back-to-back orgasms.

Once everyone left, they decided their families needed to know and Raven made Simeon promise not to tell their parents until she had a chance to call them. Now, they were on their way over to his parent's house. He'd decided to surprise them. He slanted a quick glance at Raven. She hadn't said much and he really wanted to know how she felt. Was she happy or still afraid? Though he wanted the answer, right now he thought it best not to ask. Bryson didn't want to risk his parents, particularly his mother, picking up on the tension before he and Raven talked. The less interference from his family, the better.

He parked the car in the driveway of the one-story house where he'd grown up. As always, the front yard looked freshly mowed, the edges trimmed and his mother's roses, nicely pruned. "You ready?"

Raven rotated her head in his direction. "Ready is probably not the word I'd use at this moment, but we have to tell them sooner or later. I'm still adjusting."

Bryson could tell she was overwhelmed. If he were being honest, he'd admit to teetering on the edge himself. The mere thought of caring for two babies at once would be a daunting task, but he and Raven made the best team and they could do this. He got out and went around to her side to help her. "I tell you what, when we get home, we'll call your parents, then we can shower, hop into bed and chill."

"That sounds really good," she said with a smile. "Okay, let's do this."

Taking her hand, he led her up the walk and rang the doorbell.

The door opened and his mother's eyes lit up. "Bryson, Raven, come in." She grabbed Raven and hugged her and repeated the gesture with Bryson. "Why didn't you tell me you guys were coming over, I would've cooked dinner."

"You sound just like my mom," Raven said. "But we've already eaten."

"Come on back. Your dad and I are just watching a movie."

Bryson's father stood and spread his arms when they entered the family room. "There's my favorite daughter."

Laughing, Raven stepped into his embrace. "How are you, Dad?"

"Doing well, aside from the aches and pains that go along with getting old." He turned to Bryson. "How're you doing, son?"

"I'm good."

"The center doing well?"

"It is. We're just about ready to open the new preschool, so I'm excited."

"That's wonderful, Bryson," his mother gushed. "And it's so needed."

"That's what I like to hear." His father gestured to the sofa. "Have a seat. What brings you guys by?" He resettled in his recliner, while Bryson's mother did the same in a matching one.

Bryson shared a look with Raven and she gave him a barely perceptible nod. "We wanted to let you know that you're going to be grandparents."

His mother shot up from her chair. "Are you serious? Oh, my goodness, I'm so happy! Wait until I tell all the ladies in my reading group." She did a little dance and clapped her hands.

"And we're having twins." There was stunned silence for a full minute.

His mother dropped back down in her chair and brought her hands to her mouth. "*Two* babies?"

"Two." He laughed at the stunned look on his father's face. "Dad, that's the same expression we had when we found out."

His father shook his head. "Wow. Do you have twins in your family, Raven?"

"Not that I know of, so I'm more than a little shocked."

Bryson looked at Raven. *Yeah, shocked is a good word.*

"This has been the best news," his mother said. "A double blessing." She angled her head thoughtfully. "Bryson, you know I always secretly wanted you and Raven to get together."

Bryson whipped his head around. "You never told me that."

She lifted a brow. "I just said it was a secret wish. Why would I have told you?"

Raven burst out laughing. "Thanks, Mom. I appreciate the endorsement, but did you have a specific reason why?"

"You were always so supportive and had his back, and no matter what happened, you could always put a smile on Bryson's face. I don't think either of you realized how perfect you'd be for each other."

Bryson certainly hadn't, but he did now. "You know you could've saved me years if you'd said something earlier. And you might've already had those grandmother bragging rights."

She smiled. "Probably, but you two weren't ready. Everything happens in its own time. When are my babies due?"

"Around your birthday."

"I'm going to have some March babies." Tears welled in her eyes. "I didn't think I could be any happier. You know I'm going to be praying for them to be born on my day. I need to get me a grandma T-shirt."

Bryson and Raven stared as she ran down all the grandma gear she needed to have. If the way she was going all in alarmed him, he knew Raven was probably on the verge of a serious breakdown. He covered her hand with his and gave it a comforting squeeze. When Patricia Montgomery got started there was nothing to do but wait until she finished. His father, on the other hand, sat with an amused smile. Eugene Montgomery's quiet spirit was the perfect balance to his wife's larger-than-life personality. "Mom, it's only July. You don't have to buy everything today. We don't even know what we're having yet."

She waved a dismissive hand. "I'm going on the internet tonight and see about those custom shirts. Oh, and I need to find matching outfits for my babies."

Raven's hand trembled in his.

"Um…Mom, we're going to go. We still have to call

Raven's parents and you know there's a three-hour time difference." He gently pulled Raven to her feet.

"Tell Margaret I'll call her next week, so we can compare notes."

The two women were going to give them fits. He could feel it. After rounds of hugs and goodbyes, he hustled himself and Raven out the door and into the car.

"I guess your mom's excited."

"Yeah."

"My mom is probably going to be worse. You know that offer to chill tonight?"

"Yeah?"

"I'm going to need at least three butter cookies, too."

Bryson laughed. "Anything you want, sweetheart. After having to deal with our moms, I'm going to need a couple myself." What he really needed was a double shot of something dark and strong, but he'd settle for the mouth-watering cookies. And his wife being as happy as he was about their babies.

As soon as Raven walked into the house, her phone chimed. She prayed it wasn't one of her girls. She'd have to tell them, but not tonight. Telling their parents was about all she could take. She did feel bad that Ryleigh, Quinn, Mac and Ava wouldn't know first. They were her ride-or-die sisters of the heart and they deserved to hear the news before everyone else. But there was no way they could get out of telling the guys and Simeon when they returned from the hospital. She checked the display and saw a message from Simeon wanting to know if she'd talked to their parents.

She replied: *Getting ready to call now. On overload at the moment, though.*

Simeon: *I know you'll need a moment tonight, so text me tomorrow so I know you're okay. Love you, sis, and I'm really happy for you and Bryse.*

Raven: *Love you, too.*

"Was that one of the girls?" Bryson asked.

"No. Simeon. He wanted to know if we talked to my parents."

"Do you want to wait for a while?"

"No. It's already after seven, and I just want to get it over with, so I can hop into bed with you." She needed the comfort of his strong arms around her, to reassure her everything would be okay. That they could do this. That *she* could do this. The doubts surfaced, but she shoved them back down, choosing to focus on Bryson's words, instead. *Who are you going to believe—a self-serving asshole or the man who adores you, the one who'd give his life for you and who has your back no matter what?"* Raven needed to believe him. They went upstairs to their bedroom and Raven kicked off her shoes and stretched out on the bed.

Bryson did the same and lay next to her.

She dialed her parents and put it on speaker. Her father's soothing voice came over the line and she smiled.

"Hey, baby girl. How are you?"

"Hi, Dad. I'm good. Is Mom around?"

There was a pause. "Yes, is everything alright?"

"Everything's fine." Okay, so *fine* wouldn't be the way she described everything at this moment. A better description would be shaken, stunned, freaked out and a molecule away from a major emotional shutdown.

"Okay, let me get her."

"You stay on the line, too."

"Honey, are you sure you're okay?"

"Yes, Dad."

A few seconds later, her mother picked up the line. "Hey, Raven. You're calling pretty late. What's going on?"

Leave it to her mother to get right to the heart of the matter. She tried to come up with some eloquent way of telling them. In the end, she just blurted it out. "We're having a baby."

"*Hallelujah! Yes, Lord!*" her mother screamed into the phone.

Raven jumped and rushed to turn the volume down.

"Congratulations, sweetheart," her father said. "Where's Bryson?"

"Right here, Dad."

"Congratulations, son."

"Thanks."

Margaret Holloway was still crying and babbling incoherently about everything from shopping trips to frequent visits.

"Mom." She had to call her mother's name twice more to get her attention. "There's more."

"What? Is something wrong?"

"No, Mom. It's just that we're…we're…." She felt lightheaded just having to say the words. Raven finally forced the words past her throat. "We're having twins." Just like Bryson's parents, the news caused complete silence.

As usual, her mother was the first to recover. "I think I need to lay down."

"Join the club," Raven muttered.

"I am so happy. I get *two* babies to spoil. Ooh, I can't wait to see my pretty grandbabies. Are you having the shower here or there? Hmm…it probably makes more sense to have it there. I'll have to make my flight plans and, of course, I'll come down after the babies are born to help you. I can stay two or three weeks, that way—"

Stay two or three weeks? Her eyes widened and her heart

started pounding. "Mom, I need you to slow down. I just found out today."

"Hey, Mom," Bryson said. "Raven and I would love to have you visit the babies and we'll definitely figure out how all that will work when the time comes. Right now, she and I are adjusting to the news."

She giggled. "Oh, yes. I can imagine. It is a lot to digest at once."

"My mom said she'll call you next week."

"Great. I can't wait. Pat and I have a lot to discuss."

Raven could just envision how that phone call would go. They both would probably talk over each other the entire time. "Mom, I need you to slow your roll. You're way too excited right now."

"Of course, I'm excited. Do you know how long I've been waiting to be a grandmother?"

Her father chuckled. "Raven, you know your mother."

Yes, she did. And she knew that everyone in Rosewood Heights would know by morning.

As if she'd read Raven's mind, Margaret said, "I've got to go make some calls. It's not eleven yet, so it's not too late."

"*Mom*, really? Can you not tell everyone yet? Give us at least a couple of days before you take out an ad in the paper."

"Oh, alright. But first thing Monday morning…"

Raven rolled her eyes.

Bryson chuckled, pressed a soft kiss to her lips and whispered, "It's okay, baby."

"We're going to go, Mom."

"Okay. Thanks for making my night. I love you two very much and I'm so happy for you."

"Love you, too, Mom." She disconnected, tossed the phone aside and slid down on the pillow. She groaned.

"Come here."

She rolled to her side and laid her head on Bryson's chest.

With the strong, rhythmic sound of his heart beating beneath her ear and his arms wrapped protectively around her, Raven felt the tension start to leave her body. As always when she became overwhelmed, he didn't talk. Just held her. Waiting for her to share when she was ready. She knew he had questions and was worried about how she'd taken the news. And she would tell him in a little while as soon as she figured it out. For now, she needed quiet.

Raven must have fallen asleep because when she opened her eyes the room was almost dark. She lifted her head and found Bryson was staring at her. "How long did I sleep?"

Bryson glanced over his shoulder at the nightstand clock. "About forty-five minutes. How're you feeling?"

"Better. Being here like this with you always helps."

He smiled faintly. "It helps me, as well."

"I'm still scared," she blurted. "I was just getting used to the idea of being okay with the thought of *getting* pregnant and figured by the time it happened, I'd be good."

"And now?" he asked, uncertainty lining his voice.

"Now, I think I'm blessed to have a best friend and husband who loves me. And even though I still have that fear, I want you to know that I am happy about us having these babies and I'm going to do my best to be the kind of mother they deserve."

"Raven," Bryson whispered and crushed his mouth against hers.

As she lost herself in the kiss, Raven knew everything would be okay.

Sunday morning, Raven woke up to the smell of bacon cooking. *Real* bacon. She threw back the covers and headed to the bathroom. By the time she came out, Bryson was there with a tray holding two plates.

"I thought breakfast in bed might be nice today."

"You spoil me so much." She sauntered over to where he stood and kissed him. "Good morning."

"Morning."

They climbed back in bed and devoured the eggs, bacon, grits and toast. "This was so good. Thank you."

"You're welcome."

"I needed a full stomach before calling the crew."

He stood, picked up the tray and started for the door. "Uh oh, let me leave before all the squealing and giggling starts."

"I know you didn't," she said with a laugh and threw a pillow at him, hitting him square on the side of his head. "Bullseye!"

"Hey! Crazy woman, you almost made me drop these dishes. You know what they say about payback."

Raven didn't care what they said, she was too busy laughing. She blew him a kiss. "You know I love you, baby."

"Whatever. That's not going to help you when I come for you." Bryson gave her a look that promised retribution and walked out.

Still smiling, she picked up her phone, texted Simeon to let him know all was well, then grabbed her iPad to Face-Time with her friends. As their images popped up on the screen one-by-one, Raven smiled. "Hey, sisters."

"Hey, girl," they all chorused.

"I thought I'd check in and see how the challenge is going."

Ava laughed. "She's not talking to me. Mac? Quinn? Ryleigh?"

Ryleigh was the first to respond. "My reply is the same as it was when we made that damn pact. Hell. No."

"But you agreed," Quinn said.

"That's because I was tired of your sad ass face."

Raven laughed.

"The sex is good. *Real* good," Mac said. She shrugged. "That's all I got."

"Mac, I didn't expect you'd say anything else."

Ryleigh leaned forward. "What about you, Raven, since you're all in everybody else's business."

"Let's just say I won't be the one paying for the girls trip."

"Aw, shit!" Ryleigh pumped her fist. "Bryson is the *man*."

"I'm so happy for you guys," Ava said.

"Quinn, can you not start with the tears?"

"They're happy tears, Ryleigh, and I can cry if I want to, dammit. My girl is having a baby."

"Congrats to you and Bryson." Mac tilted her head to the side and narrowed her gaze. "Hold up." A moment later, her mouth fell open. "That means your ass was already pregnant when we made the pact." She grinned.

Raven nodded. "It would've been around that time." More like the weekend before. Sex by the lake under the moonlight.

"I know Bryson is happy."

"Happy doesn't even describe my husband right now. He can't wait for the babies to be born." They all oohed and ahhed and launched into a discussion about names and baby showers. She waited to see how long it would take for them to realize she'd said *babies*.

Ava cut herself off midsentence. "Wait, wait, wait. Stop! Shut up, y'all."

"What?" Quinn said.

"I think she said babies, as in more than one."

Raven nodded. They all screamed and she covered her ears. Laughing, she said, "It took y'all long enough to hear me."

"I can't believe it. *Twins*." Mac held up her hands. "That's an entirely different thing. Are you okay, sis?"

"I have to admit, I'm a little nervous. I was already having issues about getting pregnant in the first place because—" She didn't want to bring up her ex and how she'd let his words shake her confidence, but these were her girls.

"Because what?" Ava prompted.

"Because of something Darren said." She shared the same thing that she'd told Bryson. "I know I shouldn't have let him get to me like that, but this whole motherhood thing is kind of scary."

"Say the word and I'll fly down to throat punch that sorry mutha—"

"Ryleigh!" Ava shook her head.

"What? I'm just saying. He deserves that shit for what he did."

Ryleigh did not play when it came to those in her circle and Raven loved her for it. "I'm good, Ryleigh. Anyway, I just wanted to tell you the news. Now I need to go eat the butter cookies I didn't get last night."

"I'll have a drink for you," Ryleigh said.

Raven chuckled. "Thanks. Somebody needs to do it. I love y'all." After making a promise to chat again next month, they ended the call. She placed the iPad against her heart. They said it took a village. She smiled. *I have mine.*

CHAPTER 5

The following Saturday afternoon, Raven stood in the small room with Kendrick, Bryson, Jerome and the other two groomsmen waiting for the wedding to begin. She straightened Kendrick's tie. "You look good."

"Thanks. I didn't think I'd be this nervous."

She smiled. "My mom always says the only reason you should be nervous is if you don't know what you're getting at the end of the aisle."

Bryson and Jerome laughed.

"I'll keep that in mind," Kendrick said.

"I don't think you have to worry because the woman who's coming to meet you loves you a lot. She told me so," Raven added. "You deserve this happiness." She glanced down at her watch. "Thirty minutes to go."

He hugged her. "Thanks for being the sister I've always needed. And I'm happier than I've ever been."

"Aww, that's so cute," Jerome said.

"Shut up, Rome. You know you're next."

"Ken—"

Kendrick waved a dismissive hand. "Yeah, yeah, I know.

You like your bachelor status."

"Until that bed starts to get cold at night," Bryson said with a grin.

Raven hooked her arm in Bryson's "Alright, guys. Leave Jerome alone." She leaned up to kiss Bryson. "I'm going to get my seat."

The wedding planner interrupted to pin the boutonnieres on the groom, best men and groomsmen.

Raven leaned close to Jerome. "You can fool them because they're men, but I see what they don't."

"What are you talking about?"

"You do want that forever kind of love." She smiled and patted his chest. "Don't worry. She's out there and she's going to love you like I love Bryson."

Jerome lifted a brow. "Whoa, girl. Did I miss something?"

"Nope. Just be on the lookout because she's coming."

"What are you guys talking about?" Bryson divided a speculative gaze between Raven and Jerome.

"Nothing. I was just telling him how nice he looks." She gave Jerome a conspiratorial wink and strutted out the room. Out in the hotel's covered garden space, she sat behind Kendrick's parents and took a sip of the ice cold water she'd brought. It helped with the slight nausea she had begun to have a couple of days ago. Raven hoped she didn't develop full blown morning sickness. She had too much to do and she hated vomiting as much as she did crying. And she didn't want anything to come between her and her beloved food. The realization that she was carrying two new lives inside of her had finally begun to sink in. Did she still experience bouts of doubt and fear? Yes, but not like before. She figured most new mothers felt the same. On some level, she was certain the anxiety would increase the closer she came to delivery, but with Bryson in her corner, she'd be able to handle it.

The music started and Raven rotated in her seat to watch the processional. Although the bride and groom were stunning and wedding party looked nice, Raven only had eyes for one man. He was just as handsome as he'd been on their wedding day. Throughout the ceremony, his gaze strayed to hers often. He sent a smile her way, the secret one that was reserved just for her. She responded in kind, wanting him to know that she had one that was all his, too. One filled years of unconditional friendship and unshakable love.

She refocused on the ceremony as Kendrick and Joelle spoke their vows, exchanged rings and sealed their union with a kiss. Bryson turned her way and he smiled, as if remembering their special day. She remembered, as well.

Right after the ceremony, Bryson came over to where Raven sat waiting while the wedding party took pictures. "How are you feeling?"

"Okay. The water helps."

"Do you need me to get you anything?"

Raven patted his thigh. "I'm fine, Bryse." Ever since they found out about the babies, he'd been even more protective of her. He called or texted at least once a day while she was at work to check on her and made sure she rested for a short while in the evenings. Rather than argue or fuss, she counted herself blessed and let him have his way. "Go take your pictures. I'll wait for you."

Bryson gave her a quick kiss, then went to join the group.

She watched for a while, then the July heat started getting to her. She gestured that she was going inside, reiterating that she felt fine, just hot. She wandered around to the room where the reception would be held. The space had been lavishly decorated in shades of deep purple and silver. Raven found her assigned seat, near the head table. Several other people obviously had the same idea of getting out of the heat and started trickling in. By the time the wedding party was introduced and dinner served, she was starving.

Raven happened to be seated with Kendrick's parents, so she spent time catching up with them. She and Bryson decided to wait a few weeks before sharing their news outside of their small circle, so she skipped mentioning the pregnancy. After dinner, she sat through requisite toasts, first dances and cake cutting. When it came time for the bouquet toss, she laughed until she cried when one woman did an Olympic worthy dive to catch the flowers. Next came the garter toss. Instead of throwing it, Ken walked directly over to Jerome and stuffed it the upper pocket of his suit coat.

Raven stood and clapped. "Yes!" Jerome shot her a glare similar to the one he'd given Kendrick moments before, and she continued to smile. She had never considered herself to be a romantic like Quinn, but now that she knew what true love felt like, she wanted all of her friends to experience the same.

"May I have this dance?" Bryson whispered in her ear.

Raven had been so focused on everything else, she hadn't noticed Bryson approach. "Yes." She allowed him to help her up and escort her out to the dance floor where the DJ was playing an R&B ballad. "This takes me back to our day." She laid her head on his chest.

"That was the best day of my life."

She lifted her head briefly. "Mine, too." His hands trailed down her back while his hard body moved sensually against hers, igniting a blaze. Her pulse skipped and heat spread through her.

"I love holding you in my arms, feeling your soft curves," he said against her ear as they swayed to the slow tune. "Tonight, I'm going to make love to you slowly. I'm going to touch and kiss you starting from your feet to your head. I want to taste you, savor you."

A shudder passed through Raven. She was on fire and she needed him to put it out now, not later. "How long do we have to stay?"

"Not much longer."

"Good." She stared into his eyes. "I want you to touch me, to kiss me and make love to me. I want it all. And I don't want to wait." She thought about the forty-five minute drive home and didn't think she would make it without wanting to pull off to the side of the road.

Bryson kissed her softly. "You won't have to."

He continued to tell her all the ways he planned to plea-sure her and his intense gaze had her tempted to drag him off the floor and into the nearest empty room. Hell, she'd settle for a closet at this point. "Bryson, I need you to stop playing with me."

"Baby, I plan to *play* with you all night long."

That's it! Raven stopped dancing, took his hand and nearly ran out of the ballroom.

Bryson didn't need to be persuaded to leave. His best man duties were over and the knowing smile on Kendrick's face said he understood. Raven hadn't slowed since they exited the room. "Slow down."

She eyed him. "I'll slow down once you keep every promise you made on that dance floor."

"Where are you going?"

"To the car. Where else?"

He stopped walking and chuckled. "Do you remember me saying you wouldn't have to wait?"

"Yes."

"I meant every word." Bryson changed directions and headed for the bank of elevators near the registration desk.

"What are you talking about?"

He hit the up button. "I'm talking about keeping my promises, just like you asked." The only part of the promise he might have trouble with was going *slow*. The doors opened and he gestured her forward. Inside he pushed the button for the ninth floor and they rode the car up silently. No way could he have made the drive home. Not as hard as he was at the moment. Besides, they hadn't celebrated their good news and he couldn't think of a better way than two nights in a hotel suite. No interruptions. Just the two of them. Bryson let them inside the suite.

"Whose room is this? Are we having some kind of after party with Kendrick and Joelle?"

"No. It's ours. For the next two nights. I talked to your boss and cleared it so you'll have Monday off. I thought we could use some time away."

Raven smiled. "You are the *bestest* ever."

He laughed and tugged his tie loose. "Let's see if I can live up to the hype." Bryson took his time stripping them both, then laid Raven on the king-sized bed. He placed butterfly kisses on her ankles, then kissed his way up, first one inner thigh, then the other. The way she arched and writhed, and the sweet sound of her passionate cries aroused him further. He spread her legs wider and latched on to her core, delivering on his promise to taste and savor her. He stroked her deeper, twirling and sliding his tongue throughout her wetness. "You taste so sweet, baby," he murmured. Bryson didn't stop until she climaxed.

She moaned. "Bryse."

He continued his exploration, moving upward to her belly and her breasts. He used his tongue to tease and suck, first one nipple, then the other. Already, he noticed the subtle changes. They were fuller and more sensitive. Then he trailed kisses over her chest and neck. He kissed her hungrily while holding her still trembling body. He couldn't get enough of her. Bryson gently turned her over and kissed his way down her back while caressing the firm flesh of her butt. Unable to wait any longer, he angled her hips, positioned his erection at her entrance, and gritted his teeth as he eased into her. The feel of her tightness surrounding him sent a shudder through him. They both moaned. He pulled out to the tip and plunged back in, repeating the languid movement over and over. Each time, brought him closer to the brink of ecstasy. The sounds of their breathing increased and he sped up his movements. "I can't get enough of you." He tilted her hips, never missing a beat. "I need to be deeper inside you, baby."

"Deeper, Bryse."

Bryson gripped her hips tighter and his strokes came faster. Her breath came in short gasps and she convulsed with a loud wail. "That's it. Come for me, sweetheart." He placed his thighs on either side of hers and pumped faster. She clamped down on him with her inner muscles and he cursed.

"It's your turn. Come for me, Bryse."

She did it again and electricity shot through his body. He pounded into her harder and faster and she clenched him again and again, demanding that he give her everything. As the spasms continued to wrack her body, it triggered his own release and the climax shot through him with a force that left him weak and panting. He groaned and called her name. Closing his eyes, he collapsed and shifted his body so as not to put all his weight on her.

"Bryse, you more than lived up to the hype. Fifteen minutes and we do it again?"

He laughed softly. "As many times as you want." As he'd told her, he planned to play with her all night long. He hoped they'd still be like this in the months to come.

CHAPTER 6

*R*aven was hot, fat and miserable. Her body had undergone so many changes in the past several months that she barely recognized herself. The babies seemed to be playing every sport in the book, kicked her constantly and never slept. She hadn't seen her feet in the past six weeks and she was ready for this whole pregnancy thing to be over. She'd stopped working a month ago and was bored out of her mind. There was only so much she could do walking around the house. *Two weeks to go. I can do this.*

Raven walked down the hallway—waddled would be a more accurate description—to see the finished nursery. Between their mothers and friends, she and Bryson hadn't needed to buy much. She ran her hand over the black cherry wood of the cribs that would convert to a toddler bed, daybed and a full-sized bed with a headboard and footboard. Between them were two rocking chairs and on the other side of the room, two changing tables and a large chest of drawers filled to the brim with clothes she was sure they'd grow out of before they could wear them all. She had to admit, the grandmothers were on their game.

She heard the phone ring and hurried back to her bedroom to catch it. She shook her head when she saw her mother's name on the display. It was probably the tenth time she'd called in the past three days. "Hi, Mom."

"Hi, baby. How are you feeling?"

"The same way I was the last time you called," she said with a laugh. "Nothing's changed. I'm still looking and feeling like a beached whale."

"Nonsense. You're glowing and beautiful. I just wish we lived closer so I could've have been there throughout this journey, rather than having to experience it through photos and technology." Raven had sent photos and communicated with her parent by videoconference monthly.

"I know, but just think how it would've been twenty years ago—pictures by snail mail and no FaceTime or Zoom." She opened another late baby shower gift that had arrived earlier, then headed back to the babies' room to add the swaddling blankets to the drawer.

Her sigh came through the line. "I know, I know. But these are my first grandchildren. So, have you changed your mind about us being there for the birth?"

Raven sighed. She knew the subject would come up again. She and Bryson had decided to have the first two weeks alone with the babies before having their families camping out. She figured her girls would visit soon after, but none of them would be staying over, so that didn't count as interrupting the bonding time. "Mom, we've already talked about this. Bryse and I need this time together first. And before you say anything, yes, we've told his parents the same. Simeon, too. After that, you guys are welcome to visit. Because even though I'm supposed to be all grown up, I still need my mama," she added. And she did. She considered herself to be fortunate to have a mother like Margaret Holloway, who would walk through fire for Raven, if needed.

"And I'll always be here, sweetheart. But you'd better not let Pat steal all my babies' kisses."

She laughed. "I promise they'll have some specifically for you. I love you, Mom."

"Love you, too. I'll call you soon."

Raven disconnected and smiled. She wouldn't trade her mom for the world.

"Raven. Where are you?"

She stuck her head out the door. "In the babies' room." She heard Bryson's footsteps on the stairs and a moment later, he appeared. "Hey. How'd the day go?"

"Good." Bryson leaned down and kissed her. "What about your day?"

"I'm bored as all get out and I need *your* children to chill out for at least two hours. And I just hung up with my mom...*again*."

He chuckled and wrapped his arms around her. "Your mom loves you, and in a couple more weeks you won't be bored."

"Oh, and I'm tired of being body to belly with you. I want my whole body to touch your whole body." They hadn't had sex in the last two weeks because he thought they should take it easy. Raven didn't want easy, she wanted him, and preferably, deep, fast, and hard.

"It's just for a little while longer, baby." He ran his finger over her lips. "Stop pouting."

She slapped his finger away.

Bryson smiled. "We're going out for a midweek dinner tonight."

"Do I have to put on a dress?" Thanks to Quinn, who had sent Raven multiple links for maternity clothes, Raven had a wardrobe that could have been worn during Fashion Week.

"No, but the baggy shorts and tee has to go."

She could handle that. They went back to the master bedroom and Raven changed into a charcoal colored long-sleeved ruched top and black jeans. She recombed her hair, letting the long strands hang loose between her shoulder blades, added lip gloss and her low-heeled boots, then met Bryson downstairs. He still had on the tailored slacks and dress shirt he'd worn to work.

Bryson stood at her entrance. "You look beautiful."

Even though she didn't see herself as beautiful, his intense stare made her feel that way. "Thanks." She followed him out to the car and he held the door open for her. She didn't bother to ask where they were going, but she knew whichever restaurant would have good food. She'd stuck to her normal program and hadn't gained an excessive amount of weight, which pleased her doctor. When he pulled up to *Lawry's*, she whipped her head in his direction. "This is where we had our first real date."

"I wanted to come back to where it all began to remind you of all the things I said and to let you know nothing has changed."

Emotion clogged her throat and all she could manage was a nod. *This man is going to make me cry.* He'd been messing with her tough girl image for the past three years. Raven quickly swiped at the tears before they could fall.

As he held the restaurant door open, he said, "And your tough girl status is still good."

"It better be," she said with a mock frown. The sight of rose petals scattered all over the table the hostess led them to had her status in jeopardy all over again. Over dinner, they talked, laughed and teased. "This was just what I needed, Bryse. Thank you."

"I have another surprise for you when we get home."

"What is it?"

"A surprise."

"Oh, come on. Quit playing." She leaned forward. "If you tell me, I'll have a surprise for you tonight that includes licking, sucking and more pleasure than you can stand." His eyes darkened with desire for a split second.

"Nope. Now behave and let's go."

"Party pooper." On the way out, she said, "I need to go to the bathroom first. Somebody is sitting on my bladder."

Laughing, Bryson said, "I'll have the car brought around."

"Okay." Luckily, the bathroom was empty and she didn't have to wait, a luxury she didn't have these days. Raven finished up and went out front. She didn't see Bryson or the car.

"Raven, is that you?"

She froze. Of all the restaurants in Los Angeles, this would be the one where she'd run into her ex. She barely spared him a glance. "Darren."

"I thought that was you and Bryson. I see you're still just one of the guys."

She already owed him for grabbing her and leaving her stranded, and wanted to knock him into the middle of the parking lot. She mentally counted to ten and tried to ignore him.

"If you stop hanging out with your friends, maybe you could get a man."

Raven slowly turned around and she saw his eyes widen a fraction.

"You have got to be kidding me. What man was foolish enough to knock you up?"

She clenched her fists at her sides. "You've got two seconds to get away from me."

"Or what," Darren sneered.

Without another word, she punched him in the middle of his face.

❧

Bryson jumped out of the car when he saw the man in Raven's face and her punch him.

"You *bitch*," he heard the guy say before taking a step towards her.

He was across the space in a flash. Bryson slammed the man against the wall and held him there with his forearm across the man's throat. Recognition dawned. Darren. The man who'd broken Raven's heart. The one who put his hands on her three years ago and left her to get home any way she could. The one who'd messed with his wife.

"Take your hands off me," Darren croaked, struggling and clawing to get loose.

"You put your hands on my *wife*!" He pressed his arm a little tighter across Darren's throat. "Don't you ever touch her again. Better yet, don't even let her name fall out of your mouth." Bryson exploded his fist in Darren's face and let him slump to the ground. He drew in a couple of deep breaths to regain control, then took the few steps to Raven. "Are you okay?" He palmed her face and assessed her critically. If he saw one mark, one bruise, Darren was going to need an ambulance.

Raven nodded. "Pissed, but fine."

He ran his hands up and down her arms. "Let's go home." He leaned down and told Darren, who was still on the ground moaning and clutching his face, "Remember what I said." He draped a protective arm around Raven and escorted her to the car. Once she was in safely, his heart rate started to slow. "What happened?"

"I was standing there waiting for you and he started in on the same crap he used to spew about me being one of the guys and never finding a man if I kept hanging out with you."

"And that's why you hit him?"

"No." She faced him. "He asked me what man was foolish enough to knock me up. I wasn't going to let him say shit about you."

He lifted a brow. "Since when did you start cursing?" Every now and then she let a mild curse word leave her mouth, but he couldn't remember the last time he heard that word come from her.

"Blame Ryleigh and Mac. And he deserved it." She sat back in a huff.

Bryson threw his head back and roared with laughter. That was his baby. His mother said that Raven had always had his back. Tonight she proved it without question. "Are you sure you're okay?"

"Um...I'm not sure that's the right word at the moment."

His laughter faded. "Then what's the right word."

"Labor. I think my water just broke."

It was his turn to let a curse word fly and for a few seconds, he couldn't figure out how to start the car. He'd been the calm one the entire duration of the pregnancy, but right now, *he* was the one about to lose it. He started the car and sped out of the lot. He tried to remember if he should call the doctor first or just go straight to the hospital. He opted for the latter. "But you still have two weeks left."

"I guess not," she said with a soft smile. "And remember the doctor mentioned the possibility of inducing me, depending on what she saw tomorrow."

Yes, he did recall the conversation. However, it seemed as though their babies decided to take matters into their own hands. By the time they made it to the hospital, he'd gotten himself back in control. It took over nine hours for the babies to make their entrance into the world and the entire experience took his breath away. Had either Jerome or Kendrick been there to see the tears in Bryson's eyes, Bryson's man card would've been in serious jeopardy. But he didn't care. He stroked each of their brows. His mother would be disappointed about not having her birthday grandbabies, but he had no doubt that she would get over it within seconds after seeing them. Bryson stared down at his sleeping wife. She was his shero, his best friend, his heartbeat. His forever.

EPILOGUE

*R*aven smiled down at the precious sleeping bundles in her arms and her love for them filled her heart to such magnitude, she thought it would burst. She placed a gentle kiss on each of their foreheads.

"There's my girl."

She laughed softly as Bryson entered with yet another vase of roses. "Hey. You know we're not going to have anywhere to put those soon." The hospital room was filled with them.

Bryson kissed her. "I can't help it. How are my babies?"

"Full and asleep, so they're good."

"And how's my baby?"

"Ready to go home and sleep in my own bed." She had only been there overnight, but the food left something to be desired and the hard mattress kept her tossing and turning all night.

"You'll get there soon. Did the doctor say when?"

"She said maybe tonight, since both are at the five pound mark."

"We're here!"

Raven's eyes lit up when she saw Mac, Ryleigh, and Quinn, and Ava rush in the room. "Oh, my goodness. How did you guys get here so fast?" She had planned to call them when she got home.

"Bryson sent a group text with baby pics, so we jumped on the first plane out," Mac said.

"Girl, you know we had to be here for this," Ryleigh added.

Quinn approached the bed. "I'm here to claim my godmother status."

Ava grasped Raven's hand. "They're beautiful, Sis. Now aren't you glad you took my advice to stop running."

Raven was more than glad. Had she let her fears get the best of her, she would have missed out on the biggest blessing in her life—Bryson. She glanced down. And her babies. She felt those stupid tears coming back, but she was *not* going to cry in front of her girls. That would ruin her image for sure. "I'm so glad you're here. Come meet your godson and goddaughter. Since my baby boy looks exactly like his father, we thought it only fitting to name him after Bryson. And this is Gia."

"Ooh, I want to hold them." Quinn went to wash her hands in the connecting bathroom and was back in a flash. She sat in the chair near the bed and Bryson helped transfer the babies to their godmother.

While all four women chatted with the babies, Raven smiled at Bryson and mouthed, "Thank you." She had her sweet babies, her ride-or-die sister girlfriends and the man who never stopped showing her what true love meant. She sighed with contentment. Life couldn't be any better.

COMING SOON

ONCE UPON A FUNERAL

Make sure to follow our Facebook Page for the the latest information on our upcoming work:

@onceuponaseries

ONCE UPON A BABY SERIES

EXCERPT - LOVE'S SWEET KISS (SASSY SEASONED SISTERS BOOK 1)

Nzinga Carlyle has finally gotten her life together after her divorce and is happily single. However, the moment she sees her teen crush at her high school reunion, old feelings start to rise. Nzinga isn't sure she's ready to move forward, although she can't deny the attraction between them. And after one sweet kiss, she has to decide how far she wants the relationship to go.

Byron Walker can't believe his good fortune when he runs into the woman who stole his teenage heart. Once he realizes their chemistry is still explosive, he vows not to let Nzinga get away a second time. Circumstances forced them apart over thirty years ago, but Byron intends to show her they were always meant to be.

CHAPTER 1

*N*zinga dropped her purse on the bed and kicked off her shoes. The day had been a long one and she'd barely had time breathe. The office had been short one pediatrician and, rather than cancel the patients, she and the physician's assistant had seen them all. Since it was Friday, she would have the weekend to recover, and she couldn't think of a better way to unwind than to hang out with her girls. She went to the drawer and pulled out a pair of shorts and a tee. Although the calendar had just changed to June, the Sacramento temperatures had already climbed well into the eighties and nineties.

After a quick shower, she backed out of her driveway and made the thirty-minute drive from West Roseville to Donna's house in Natomas. When she got there, she saw that Max and Val had already arrived.

Donna answered the door within seconds after Nzinga rang the bell. "Hey, girl. Come on in." They shared a quick hug.

Nzinga followed her back to the family room. When she

entered, Val and Max stood and started cheering. She shook her head at their antics.

"How does it feel to be a free woman?" Max asked, bringing Nzinga in to a warm embrace.

"Better than I ever thought." She had received her divorce decree in the mail earlier in the week after almost two years of hassling with her ex. As a result, her three friends were hosting the celebration. "If it hadn't been for Donna finding out all that crap, I might still be trying to get out." She hugged Val. "It also helped that I had the best attorney in the country."

Val laughed. "I'd like to say you're lying, but..." She shrugged.

"Hey, if you don't brag on yourself, who will?" Max said.

"Amen!" they chorused.

Max snapped her fingers. "Speaking of crap, did you see Melvin's bid for governor fizzed out?"

Donna snorted. "Hard to run on a campaign of family when you have a baby mama and several side pieces." The women cracked up.

A few weeks ago, his photo had popped up on the news. Nzinga had changed the channel before the reporter could say one word. She could care less about him or his campaign. After the laughter subsided, they all took seats. She crossed her legs at the ankles. "What's for dinner? I'm starving. We had back-to-back patients today and I didn't finish lunch."

Max raised her hand. "Same here. I usually eat on the way to the next client's house, but they were all in the same vicinity and could only get in a couple of bites at a time." Maxine worked as a home-based pediatric occupational therapist, seeing clients birth to three years old. She often joked that she played for a living.

Donna smiled. "We're having Nzinga's favorite lasagna. I knew I wouldn't have time to make it, so I asked Monique to do it. She should be here in a few minutes." Monique was Donna's twenty-six year-old daughter and the goddaughter of the other three women. "The salad is done and the garlic bread won't take long. In the meantime, we need wine."

"You ain't said nothing but a word." Val jumped up and led the way to the kitchen. After all their glasses were filled, she lifted her glass. "To Nzinga. May she enjoy her newfound freedom."

"And may she find a sexy brother to help her get her freak on," Max added, which brought on another round of laughter.

"Crazy woman." They touched glasses and sipped. Nzinga shook her head. It had been so long, she probably wouldn't even remember *how* to get her freak on. That wasn't on her radar. For now, she just wanted to savor her newfound peace.

"Dinner's here!"

They all turned at the sound of Monique's voice as she entered the kitchen carrying a casserole dish.

Monique set the container on the stove. "I can't believe y'all started without me."

Donna snorted. "What do you mean started without you?"

She kissed her mother's cheek. "Aw, Mom. I am old enough to have wine." Turning, she greeted Nzinga with a strong hug. "Auntie N, congratulations on finally being rid of Mr. Meanie."

Nzinga chuckled. Growing up, Monique had always said Melvin was mean and grouchy. "Thanks, baby."

She repeated the gesture with Val and Max, then asked Max, "Have you talked to Dion?"

Pain crossed Max's features. "Not since Christmas." Max had been estranged from her twenty-three year-old son, Dion since divorcing his father six years ago. Max's ex had cheated on her and spun it to insinuate that she had been the one. Dion had taken his father's side and, outside of telling her son that she had been faithful to his father, had chosen not to give the then seventeen year-old the proof she had of his father's infidelity.

Monique rolled her eyes. "He is such a butthead. Do you want me to knock some sense into him?" The two had grown up together and Monique treated Dion like a younger brother.

Max smiled. "No. Hopefully, he'll come around on his own."

"Let me know if you change your mind."

"Okay, enough of that," Donna said as she slid a pan with the garlic bread into the oven. "The bread should be done in a few minutes, then we can eat. Monique, can you set the table for me?"

"Sure, Mom. I'll need an extra piece of that garlic bread as payment, though," she added with a little laugh as she went about the task.

Nzinga reached for the bowl of salad. "I'll take this to the dining room."

Val snatched it. "You just get to enjoy yourself tonight as the guest of honor, so sashay your behind on over to the table and sit." She waved a hand toward the dining room.

"Fine with me." She topped off her wine, spun on her heel and with an exaggerated sway of her hips, strutted out, leaving a trail of laughter from her friends. Nzinga didn't know what she'd do without them. They had seen each other through every trial and triumph and she couldn't have asked for better friends. She recalled the nights she cried over the demise of her marriage and how one or more of them had stayed with her for hours. Because Max had gone through the same thing, the two of them often consoled each other. A few minutes later, all the food was placed on the table and they started in on the meal. Nobody's lasagna recipe could top Donna's. "Monique, you have your mother's recipe down to a tee."

Smiling, Monique said, "Thanks. I watched her for years, trying to perfect it."

They ate in silence for a few minutes before Valina said, "Nzinga, you're free just in time for the reunion." Their thirty-fifth class reunion would take place in three weeks.

"*Free* being the key word. I'm enjoying my life the way it is and have no plans to change it. Besides, I am too old for games."

"Old? Who's old?" Max asked. "We're not old, just *seasoned.*"

Nzinga lifted her glass in a mock toast. "Okay, I'll go with that." That statement brought on more laughter.

"I like it," Monique said. "Seasoned sisters. Wait, no, it's needs a little more pizzazz." She made a show of thinking, then grinned. "I've got it. *Sassy* seasoned sisters. Ooh, I should get you all T-shirts to wear to the class reunion. That would be so cool."

"Hey, I kind of like that."

"Max, don't encourage her." Donna stared at her daughter. "Don't you have a date with your fiancé or something?"

Monique smiled sweetly. "Nope. I made sure my evening was free because I didn't want to miss out on all this wisdom. I need to make sure I have all the do's and don'ts of this adult life."

"You're in the right place, baby." Max held up her wine. "To us sassy, seasoned sisters. May we dispense wisdom to youngsters everywhere."

"Amen!" Val said, touching her glass to Max's. They all followed suit. "Now, back to the reunion. I'm kind of looking forward to it. They're going to try to resurrect the jazz band."

"Are you going to play?" Donna asked.

"Yes, ma'am. I've already got the drum set up and have been dusting off the cobwebs. Lamont reached out to me on social media and said all twelve of us had agreed. The first practice is tomorrow."

Nzinga finished chewing her food and laughed. "I still remember the day you marched up to the band director and asked why there were only boys in the jazz band and told him you wanted to play drums."

Donna took up the story. "And the look on Desmond's face when you played him under the table during the drum-off for the position. He hated you until the day we graduated. Probably still does."

"I would've gone easy on him, but he tried to get in my face, talking about I needed to just worry about playing the bells." Val had played in the percussion section of the symphonic band, but had taken drum lessons from the age of seven and played with her older brothers. "Hmm...I wonder if he'll show up."

Nzinga eyed her. "Don't you get out there starting mess."

"I don't plan to start anything." She shrugged. "I was just wondering. Aside from him, I am looking forward to seeing a few people."

"And there are some who I'd rather not see," Max said. "Like creepy Calvin."

Nzinga frowned. "That boy was always trying to touch or kiss somebody."

"Well, if he tries it now, I will break him in half," Donna tossed out. The former police officer and Army veteran had a black belt in karate.

Max pointed her fork in Donna's direction. "You've got that right."

Monique's mouth fell open. "See, this is exactly why I stayed. I thought you guys were all sweet and now I find out that y'all are gangsta."

Donna rolled her eyes. "Girl, eat your food and hush."

She giggled and brought a forkful of lasagna to her mouth.

"At any rate, it should be fun," Nzinga said. "It looks like the committee planned it well." Friday night would be the opening activities with a casual dinner, Saturday had a family picnic during the day and formal dinner in the evening.

Max leaned back in her chair. "Nzinga, I wonder what happened to that guy you liked when we were freshmen."

Her brows knitted together. "What guy?"

"You know…his brother was in our biology class and was your partner on that big project we had to do," Val said. "What was his name?" She tapped her fingers on the table. "Wesley. That's it. But I can't remember his older brother's name."

"Byron," Nzinga said far softer than she intended. She hadn't thought of him in years. When her parents found out about them, their budding relationship was over before it got started. They had no intentions of allowing their fifteen-year-old daughter to date an eighteen-year-old *man* on his way to college in a few months. "I can't see why he would be there, since he's three years older than us."

"The family picnic, remember?" Max said with a sly smile. "Go ahead and admit it. You know you want to see what he looks like now."

"I'm not admitting anything. I'm sure he probably doesn't even remember me." However, she did think it would be nice to see him. Just to catch up, or at least that's what she told herself.

~

"What's up, teach?" Byron Walker eased around a slow-moving car on the freeway.

Wesley Walker laughed. "Well if it isn't my lazy older brother."

"Don't hate. You're just mad you still have to punch the clock every morning. And I'm not the one who only works nine months out of the year. I gave Uncle Sam over thirty years of getting up at oh-dark-hundred, so I'm entitled to a little relaxation." He had retired from the military a year ago and was enjoying his life. The only thing that would have made it sweeter was if he had someone to enjoy it with.

"I need these three months after dealing with a bunch of high schoolers in the classroom. Anyway, what's up?"

"Just checking in and seeing if you're up for a visit."

"You're in town?"

"I will be in about an hour. I was in Lake Tahoe doing some fishing." Byron woke up Monday morning and decided to make the drive from Los Angeles to Lake Tahoe. He secured a hotel, left the next morning and spent three days just enjoying the scenery. He didn't catch any fish, however. His family lived in the Sacramento area and he hadn't seen his niece and nephew in months. Since his mother had been on his case about not staying in touch, he figured he could spend a few days visiting.

"Why didn't you tell me you were up this way?"

"I'm telling you now. Are you going to be around this weekend?"

"Actually, our class reunion starts tonight, so Loren and I are going. The kids are going to be out with friends, but tomorrow there's a family picnic, so you'll definitely have to come with us. How far away are you?"

"About forty minutes."

"Oh, well, come on over. The activities don't kick off until seven and it's only two now. You can get a chance to see the kids before they leave."

"Sounds good. See you in a few." Byron made the

remainder of the drive to Folsom with the smooth sounds of
Boney James to keep him company. As soon as the door
opened, his twenty-year-old niece, Anissa leaped into his
arms.

"Uncle Byron!"

"Hey, baby girl," he said with a laugh. She didn't stand
more than five feet, two inches, taking after her mother, and
still exuded the same level energy she'd had as a little girl. He
kissed her temple and set her on her feet. "How's college
life?"

"Too much work. I'm so glad it's summer."

"Hi, Unc."

Byron did a fist bump with his seventeen-year-old
nephew, Gabriel. "How's it going? Ready for senior year?"

Gabriel grinned. "Been ready."

He smiled at his brother. "What's up, little brother?" In
addition to being three years older than Wesley, Byron also
eclipsed his brother's six-two height by two inches and never
missed an opportunity to point it out.

"Sleeping in," Wesley answered with a chuckle. "Retire-
ment looks good on you. Come on in. You want something
to eat or drink?"

"Nah, I'm good. Where's Loren?" He followed Wesley
back to the family room and sat on the sofa.

He shook his head. "She had to get her hair done, nails
done, feet done…and something else she said. With the list of
things she rattled off, it'll be a miracle if she makes it back
before it's time to leave."

Byron laughed.

"You're laughing, but you wouldn't be if you had a
woman."

"Maybe, maybe not." Byron had a list of accomplishments,
but the one thing he wished he could have added to the list
was a family. Being in the military made it difficult to find a

woman willing to deal with the multiple deployments. He'd come close a couple of times, but the relationships fizzled out before they could make it to the altar. Now, at almost fifty-seven, he'd just about given up on finding someone to share his life.

"How long are you planning to be here?"

"Probably until Monday or Tuesday, if you don't mind putting up with me."

"Not at all. Does Mom know you're in town?"

"No, and since you guys will be out tonight, I might head over there."

"You know Friday is her bingo night and she doesn't cancel going unless it's absolutely necessary."

"I know. I'll call her in a few minutes to see what she and Dad are doing tonight, but I'm not going to mention I'm here. I want to surprise them."

Wesley laughed. "Good luck with that."

They spent a few minutes catching up, then he called his parents. "Hey, Mom," he said when she answered.

"Byron. How are you, baby?"

"I'm good."

"You know we haven't seen you since Christmas and it's almost summer. With you being retired, I figured we'd get a chance to see you a little more often."

"Mom—"

"You might as well still be in the Army going on all those deployments."

He sighed and glared at Wesley, who was doubled over in his chair trying not to laugh out loud. When Naomi Walker got started, the only thing to do was sit and wait until she finished. "Mom, I promise I'll visit soon. I know this is your bingo night and you'll be leaving in a few minutes." She was usually out the door by four o'clock and his father left on his own for dinner.

"I'm not going tonight. Your Aunt Lee asked me to go with her to her doctor's appointment. I don't know why she needed to go on a Friday afternoon. She knows I have somewhere to be," she fussed.

Byron chuckled. "I'm sure all that money will be there waiting on you next week."

"It better be because I've been on a winning streak." There was a pause on the line and muffled voices. "Your aunt is here. Don't make me have to send out a posse to find you."

"I won't, Mom. Tell Dad and Aunt Lee I said hello. Love you."

"Love you, too, honey."

He disconnected and shot another lethal glare at his brother. "Shut up, Wes. I don't want to hear one word."

Wesley burst out laughing. "Man, I wish you could've seen your face. I knew Mom was going to be all over you."

"Just tell me about the damn reunion."

It took a moment for him to stop laughing before he could talk. He finally composed himself enough to speak. "Like I said earlier, tonight is just a welcome dinner and tomorrow night is a formal one, which is why my wife has spent more money in the past week than she has all year."

Byron smiled. "She just wants to look good."

"No, she said she wants to make sure all those hussies who had a thing for me in high school know that they still don't have a chance."

It was his turn to laugh. "I love my sister-in-law. I just wish I could be there to see it play out."

"You can tomorrow if you join us for the family picnic. Speaking of women, I'm sure Darlene Butler would be happy to see you. She wanted you bad."

He made a face. "If she is, she'll be still wanting me until hell freezes over."

"Aw, come on, big brother. She might've changed by now."

"I doubt it." Their senior year, Byron had been the varsity basketball captain and Darlene the head cheerleader. Somehow, she had fixed in her mind that they should date and go to the prom together and had difficulties understanding he wasn't interested in doing either. The phrase "mean girl" came into existence because of her, and, back then, he'd had neither the time or inclination to deal with her foolishness. Still didn't.

"I thought you said you were trying to find a woman."

"I am, but she could never fit the bill." Yes, he continued to hold a slim hope of finding that one special person, but he wasn't desperate.

"What about my old biology lab partner, Nzinga Carlyle?"

Byron sat up straight. He had been fascinated by her back then, but with him being three years older, their parents had forbidden the relationship. He always wondered what would have happened had they been allowed to date. "I wouldn't mind catching up with her. She's probably married with a few kids like she wanted."

"Actually, she never had children. She was married to a guy on the city council, but I think they're divorced now."

"Hmm." This impromptu trip home might turn out better than he thought.

CHAPTER 2

"**I** can't believe all the people who showed up for this picnic," Nzinga said as she, Val, Donna and Max entered their high school campus. The grassy area was filled with blankets, beach chairs and canopy shades.

"Maybe we should've gotten here a little earlier. I hope we can find a spot." Val pointed. "Look, there's an area over to the right."

The women quickened their steps to claim the spot and made it just before another group got there. They spread out the large quilt, raised the easy up shade and set up their beach chairs.

"I don't know why we needed to bring chairs, since we have the quilt," Donna said.

Max stretched her legs out. "Because I sit on the floor all week. Today, I want to be an adult and sit on a chair."

"Yeah, well, nobody told you to get a job playing with babies. If you wanted to be an adult, you should have chosen a different field."

"Shut up, Miss Rambo."

Donna smiled. "Damn straight."

Nzinga shook her head. These women filled her life with so much joy.

"Love the shirts!" a guy passing called out.

True to her word, Monique had designed gray tees with the words "Sassy Seasoned Sisters" written in a fancy font. She'd also added rhinestones because, according to her, they needed a little bling.

"Well, if it isn't the four Musketeers."

They all stood to greet Lamont Johnson, the jazz band's keyboardist and leader.

"Y'all haven't aged a day in thirty-five years."

"Please," Nzinga said. "It's too early in the day for lying." He'd added a good fifty pounds to his former string bean frame, but his smile and easygoing manner hadn't changed.

"I came to get my girl. We're going to start the music in about thirty minutes."

Val retrieved her drumsticks from her bag and held them up. "I'm ready."

"You know Desmond's here, and when he heard the band was playing, he had the nerve to ask could he sit in as drummer."

Max folded her arms. "And when you told him Val was playing?"

Lamont laughed. "Stomped off just like he did the first time. I'll see you over there in a minute, Val. Good seeing you ladies."

"Same here," they chorused.

Because of where they were seated, they had a good view of the mock stage. Confident that their belongings would be safe, the four women slung their purses on their shoulders and went over to get something to drink.

"I should've known she'd be one of the first persons we'd see today," Max grumbled.

Nzinga glance up to see Cassandra Butler headed their

way with the same stuck-up crew she'd hung out with in high school. Cassandra had never liked her and Nzinga had no idea why. But she figured that was a long time ago and water under the bridge.

"Hey, Valina, Maxine and Donna," Cassandra said as soon as she approached. She looked Nzinga up and down with disdain. "I see y'all are still hanging out with trash."

Nzinga had been determined to take the high road, but this heifer was going to make her lose all sense of decorum. She gave Cassandra a false smile. "I see you still are trash."

The two women with Cassandra nearly choked on their drinks. Cassandra took a step.

She lifted a brow. *I know she's not.*

Cassandra opened her mouth, then closed it and stormed off, her two minions following.

"I'm glad she decided not to cause a scene," Val said. "Maybe she's grown up some."

Max shook her head. "Nah, sis, that was a business decision. She remembered what happened the last time she tried to get in Nzinga's face."

Donna smiled. "Yeah, girl. She might still think she's all that, but she's not stupid."

Nzinga didn't care about the reason, she just hoped the woman kept her distance for the remainder of the weekend. In their freshman year of high school, Cassandra had made a habit of harassing Nzinga almost daily for a week. Nzinga grew tired of trying to be tactful and the next time Cassandra walked up, intending to start trouble, Nzinga dropped her with one punch, then walked away. "I'm not going to spend my time thinking about that crazy woman. We came here to enjoy ourselves, so let's do it." After getting bottles of tea, she, Donna and Max headed back to their spot, while Val went to join the band.

The band took them back, playing everything from

smooth jazz, to the R&B songs that had been popular during that time—"Cutie Pie" by One Way, "Forget Me Nots" by Patrice Rushen and "Take Your Time" by The S.O.S. Band—and had everyone on their feet dancing.

"Desmond doesn't look too happy," Donna said with a little laugh, pointing to where he stood near the stage glaring, no doubt, at Val as she flipped her sticks and never missed a beat.

Nzinga playfully bumped her shoulder. "I wouldn't either, if a *girl* could wipe the floor with me on the drums."

They launched into Earth, Wind and Fire's Shining Star and Max threw her hands in the air. "*Yaassss!* This is my *jam!*"

Apparently, that feeling was shared by everyone gathered —young and old—if the sheer volume of shouts that went up were any indication. At the end of the song, the audience all joined in to sing the final refrain acapella.

Nzinga clapped along with the crowd when it was over. "Oh, my goodness. They were fabulous. I didn't realize Val had kept up with her playing."

"Neither did I," Max said. "Girlfriend needs to put her pumps to the side and take this show on the road."

"No lie."

Donna elbowed Nzinga. "Girl, look who's coming this way."

She turned in the direction Donna gestured and saw Wesley Walker approaching with a man who she would recognize anywhere. Her heart started pounding just like it did the first time she'd seen him at their house when she and Wesley were working on a biology project. Byron stood six feet, four inches, had smooth, dark caramel skin and muscles for days. But it was his light brown eyes that had totally captivated her. And every other girl at the school. The way he stared at her now still had her mesmerized.

Max scooted close to her and whispered, "Honey, that

man is even finer than he was then. I sure hope he's single, especially since he can't seem to take his eyes off you. And that salt and pepper beard...*sexy*!" She cleared her throat and opened her arms. "Wesley Walker, the smartest guy in the world. How are you?"

Wesley laughed and embraced Max. "I don't know about that, but I'm good." He repeated the gesture with the other women, including Val, who'd just joined them. Then he placed his arm around a woman. "This is my beautiful wife, Loren."

Loren smiled easily and reached out to shake each of their hands. "I've heard a lot about you all over the years."

They all greeted Loren and Nzinga said, "I hope nothing bad."

"Not about you ladies, but I have heard a few stories about some others," she said conspiratorially.

Wesley chuckled. "Don't get her started." He introduced his two children. "I don't know if you all remember my brother, Byron. Lucky him, he came up for a visit just in time to attend this shindig."

"Who could forget the varsity basketball captain who led our team to the first championship in over a decade?" Donna said.

Byron smiled. "It's nice to see you ladies again." He turned to Nzinga and grasped her hand. "It's been a long time, Nzinga."

"Yes, it has." She ignored the knowing looks on her friends' faces. Nzinga thought herself far past the age of being affected by a man. But the mere touch of Byron's hand on hers made her pulse skip and had her heart beating at a pace that had to be dangerous. She couldn't remember the last time any man made her feel this way.

ABOUT THE AUTHOR

Sheryl Lister is a multi-award-winning author and has enjoyed reading and writing for as long as she can remember. She is a former pediatric occupational therapist with over twenty years of experience, and resides in California. Sheryl is a wife, mother of three daughters and a son-in-love, and grandmother to two special little boys. When she's not writing, Sheryl can be found on a date with her husband or in the kitchen creating appetizers. For more information, visit her website at www.sheryllister.com.

Her Passionate Promise

Love's Sweet Kiss (Sassy Seasoned Sisters #1)

Never Letting Go (Carnivale Chronicles)

CPSIA information can be obtained
at www.ICGtesting.com
Printed in the USA
LVHW020846150621
690261LV00001B/189

9 781733 867054